It's Never
Over When
It's Over

ISBN: 1452841748
ISBN-13: 9781452841748

It's Never Over When It's Over

Gene Schwarz

For my Love

Joan

Acknowledgements

Many thanks to my friends who offered their encouragement, critical eye, advice and love. I take full responsibility for the finished product, so I leave you with my love, gratitude and the gift of anonymity.

Preface

Trauma is part of living. In fact, if you met someone in the last decade of their life and they had no scars to show, you could bet they either tip-toed through the land of the living or are blessed with the rose colored filters acquired with age.

The manageable and unavoidable traumas of living teach us what not to touch, how to avoid a fall, where we start and leave off, who to love and who to avoid. We usually think of them as bumps along the road, balanced by what we learn from what we experience and the joys and love that may come our way.

Then there are the traumas that are so massive that the scars are deeply embedded in our souls. Often they heal and just as often they lie dormant, waiting for that touch that will ignite the spark that brings them back to life, to be endured once more and perhaps presenting another chance of mastery.

I've written a fictional account of Adam Burn's quest for inner peace and resolution of the trauma of war. In the 1960's, the disabling symptoms were known as a Traumatic Neurosis of War, and now, just as disabling, Post Traumatic Stress Disorder. In my practice of psychiatry and psychoanalysis, I've had the opportunity to meet and work with some courageous people who have fought through their own unique wars, on their private battlefields. All the fictional characters of this novel spring from one source and so are brought to life on these pages from the stores of my personal and professional life.

Gene Schwarz, MD
May 17, 2010

The phone didn't just ring in the on-duty room of University Hospital. It was a loud clang, like the opening bell in Friday Night Fights. It was before the day of personal pagers and God forbid a sleep-deprived resident would sleep through a call. The insistent clang pierced the blanket that Adam Burns had pulled over his head and the pillow that covered his ears left a lot to be desired. At the first sound, he bolted out of bed, his feet planted on the cold floor, with a death grip on the phone. He could hear a distant voice calling his name and finally realized it was coming from the receiver he held at his side.

"Dr. Burns... Dr. Burns... are you there?"

"Yeah... barely."

"There's a psych patient here that you need to see, Stat."

He mumbled, "Yeah... Stat," and slammed the phone down, pissed at the imperious tone of the command. He splashed cold water on his face, and started to laugh, "I guess a junior psychiatric resident doesn't rate a salute from the desk clerk of the ER."

Adam could smell something awful as he approached the front desk and was immediately pointed to the treatment room which was the farthest away from the sensitive noses of the ladies in white. When he opened the door he felt like someone had just smothered him in the most foul smelling bowel movement imaginable. He completely lost any semblance of professional presence and gagging, with eyes burning, blurring his vision he blurted,

"Holy shit... someone smells like they rolled in a pile of it," and then he vomited in the wastepaper basket with some spattering over his white shoes. He heard a snicker from what looked like a giant turd strapped to a gurney parked along the wall.

Still stunned by the smell, he didn't see any humor in the situation, and snapped, "What's so fucking funny... why the fuck are you covered with shit?"

From this man, coated in filth, came an educated eloquent reply, which almost elevated the moment into a less odorous social setting. His tone was a caricature of feudal nobility with an unmistakable English accent.

"Well young doctor I wasn't laughing at you but rather sighing with relief... I finally found someone I could trust." He raised his head and looked Adam over from head to toe, coming to rest on his groin. "You have a straight penis... if you ignored the smell in the room I wouldn't be talking to you now... when you take the restraints off I'd give you a great big hug like I did to that fat ass nurse with the crooked vagina who talked to me as if I was a little kid who had an accident."

Adam was slowly regaining his professional posture when he started to gag precipitating another trip to the wastepaper basket. He had to remind himself that he had taken an oath to help people and do no harm. It took wrapping this guy up in plastic and dumping him in the river, off the table. He splashed his face, rinsed his mouth and wondered what the hell he was doing there. He suppressed a laugh, but the voice on the gurney didn't miss a beat.

"You're laughing young doctor," and then the cultured English accent turned into the voice of a hit man for the mob, "So what's so fucking funny?"

Adam heard his own words hurled back at him by this man of many voices. The smell was eclipsed by an echoing silence. Finally, Adam said,

"You must be terrified out of your mind if you'd smear yourself with feces just to keep everyone away."

Adam saw tears slowly making their way down the mound of crud caked on his cheeks and heard a little boy sob, "You don't know how it feels when your own family is out to kill you."

Adam resisted the stereotypic psychiatric retort of telling him, he understood how he felt. He really didn't, and didn't understand why he chose to cover himself with feces as a protection from danger. It certainly wouldn't stop a bullet. All Adam knew was this man was making a big stink over something, and so he waited, while trying not to breathe. The sobs went on for what seemed like an eternity, then a teasing tone rose from the mound on the gurney.

"I'm sorry...I know I smell terrible...I'm used to it and you know what they say about your own shit smelling like roses." An explosive maniacal laugh changed the tone once again as this man broke into a broad grin revealing discolored teeth. The laugh came to an abrupt end and the smile vanished as quickly as it appeared. "I'm frantic...I don't know what to do. I'm tired...I don't want to run anymore...I almost don't care whether I live or die. I can't go on like this." He stared at the ceiling then slowly turned toward Adam, and in a drama-coated deep baritone announced,

"My name is Thomas Wittenbourne." There was a long silence letting the name sink in and take hold. Then the little boy asked, "Can you help me?"

Adam hearing the name Wittenbourne, first thought this man is manic and grandiose, but if he was telling the truth he's a member of a family of wealth and power. Immense wealth and power. The kind that can make presidents as well as turn a first year psychiatric resident into a shriveled insignificant — the power to take a contract out on anyone they chose to.

The agony on this man's face showed through the veil of debris, and a desperate cry brought Adam back to the moment.

"Please help me."

Adam didn't know how to help him or even if he could, but he knew he couldn't stand the smell much longer.

"Tom…is it OK to call you Tom?" He nodded. "I don't know if I can help you or not…all I know is I can't stand this smell much longer. I know you're terrified and I'll work my ass off to try to help you if you level with me…I'll take the restraints off if you promise not to give me a hug and promise to take a shower."

In the midst of sobs of relief Tom blurted, "I promise," then in a menacing tone added, "It's a deal as long as no one but you knows who I am." Adam's larcenous soul allowed him to agree, knowing he would break his promise in a heart beat, if he thought it necessary.

Adam got two mental health aides from the ward. They all donned gowns, masks and gloves to help Tom to the ward and showers. On the way out of the ER a lovely red-headed resident gave Adam a thumbs-up and he thought he would check her out later to see if that was just a thumbs-up or a thumbs-up. He admitted Tom under the name of Exxes which he thought was kind of creative and Tom thought was funny. The man had a sense of humor which was a plus and he kept his promise about no hugs and a shower.

It was pushing four in the morning by the time Adam got back to his room, stuffed his clothes in a laundry bag hoping to seal off the smell, and immersed himself under a hot shower. The smell clung to the innards of his nose and throat which drove him to snort some water. That sent a blaze of fire through his sinuses and he thought he should've wrapped Tom in plastic and dumped him in the river. The smell was lingering in the recesses of his brain when he finally crawled into bed. The blanket and pillow were in place anticipating the inevitable clang signaling the next round.

That's the way he thought about things. Everything was a fight, another round or at the very least a challenge. A smug-engaging humor served as a way to connect without the vulnerability that came with intimacy, and helped to mask the wounds and simmering rage he had learned to live with. Getting back to sleep was the immediate challenge. He always anticipated the dreams that would bring him back to Korea. When he was on the wagon, which lately was most of the time, he had awful dreams. Almost every night. Some he would remember and some he would wake up in a sweat, his heart pounding and yelling and cursing. All the dreams were back in Korea. Mortars, grenades, a lot of noise and loud fire. When the dreams started piling up he'd go on a weekend drunk. Two days of heavy drinking, some dancing and some fucking, would take care of the dreams for a week or two.

It seemed like two minutes ago when the clang sounded, signaling the start of another round. He groped for the phone and heard the voice of Vic Fuerte, the chief resident.

"Adam where the hell are you… we're ready to start morning rounds."

"OK…Sorry…I overslept. I'll be there in a few minutes."

Adam didn't break any records getting dressed and when he got to the resident's lounge, Vic was clearly annoyed. Adam kept him waiting a bit longer as he poured himself a cup of coffee and picked up the last doughnut. Parked at the table he managed one sip of coffee before the questions started. It didn't take long to fill his fellow residents in on his night on call. Tom Exxes was the only psych patient who came into the ER and the wards were quiet.

"I don't know anything about this man except he had coated himself with feces and he's terrified of his family. When I first came into the ER you could smell him. He was in the treatment room furthest from the front desk and the charge nurse was off changing her clothes and taking a shower." Everyone laughed when he told them Tom thought the nurse was patronizing and he gave her a hug as a show of his gratitude. "When I walked in the room I felt infiltrated with shit…I gagged and vomited and said something like he smelled like he rolled in a pile of shit…he was laughing when I was vomiting…I said something like what's so fucking funny and why the fuck are you covered with shit…at that point I realized he was not just laughing but also sobbing…that's when he told me that his family was out to kill him."

Vic said, "Even though he was making you sick you responded empathically and it allowed him to trust you."

It didn't sound to Adam like Vic was on the same planet. "Vic I didn't feel empathic at the time and it doesn't sound empathic to me now. I was hardly able to stay in the room with him and I was pissed at him…looking back on it I know he knew I was angry and my being up-front with it was what let us connect…I also didn't run out of the room although I was tempted." Adam tuned out the rest of the guessing about the meaning of Tom covering himself with his own feces and they all had a go at the straight penis and crooked vagina. Everyone added their two cents. Adam was thinking about getting some breakfast before meeting with Tom.

Vic had one last question. "What's Tom's real name?"

The bell went off and another round was about to begin. "I gave him my word I would keep that confidential until we both agreed what to do about it."

Vic wasn't happy about the agreement Adam made with his patient. Vic's tone made the point that he was the chief resident, and patients should be admitted under their real name.

"You're colluding with a man who is clearly psychotic. It's not going to be helpful in his recovery if he knows he can manipulate you."

"Vic I'm not being manipulated…it was a choice I made. I didn't want to take the chance this man was telling the truth when he said his family was out to kill him." Vic was silent and Adam stood his ground. "Tom may be psychotic but he understands I gave him my word. If I go back on it I'll lose him." Adam stood, tossed his cup in the wastebasket and all six-foot-three of him looked down at his chief resident. "I'll see Tom this morning and I'll let you know what happens."

It was pretty ballsie for a first year resident on the job for less than a month, but Adam wasn't into caving in. When he left active duty he told himself that he was through taking orders that made no sense to him. He wasn't about to be pushed around by anyone. It made med school both a joy and a challenge. People respond differently when they know they can't intimidate you, but some never give up trying.

He got some bacon and eggs, another cup of coffee, while keeping track of time so he'd get to a 10 o'clock appointment with his shrink. He rode a 600 cc Ariel, a British bike, and could manage to get uptown through traffic in about twenty minutes without killing himself There were only a few near misses in the year he'd been seeing Dr. Steven Goodman. He started with Dr. G the week he began a rotating internship. He was smoking like it was going out of style and boozing it up on the weekends which often spilled over into the rest of the week. The on call schedule was interfering with his drinking and he was getting shaky inside when he tried to stop the alcohol. Goodman had the rep as a master clinician and it didn't take him long to zero in, especially after he heard Adam's dreams.

He said, "Adam, we just met and I don't know you, but it doesn't take much of a psychiatrist to know you're suffering from a traumatic neurosis...I bet you've been plagued by these dreams for years." He rattled off a bunch of other symptoms he thought Adam might have when he was interrupted by Adam's plea.

"That's enough Doc. Enough." The room was quiet. Adam said, "I think I'm crying." There was no sign of tears. His eyes moistened a bit. He felt the tears inside. A silent private cry. "I don't ever remember crying." As if his crying was visible. Dr. Goodman could only imagine what was going on in this man, so tortured inside, and so frightened of losing control.

That night Adam had the most peaceful sleep in years. The dreams were persistent though — as soon as he thought he had them beat they came thundering back. Even with the dreams he was doing better. He got to the point where he not only looked forward to his therapy hour, but thought about asking for extra sessions. One day when Adam was talking about one of his dreams he called Dr. Goodman, Doc. Dr. Goodman broke in with,

"Adam, I would like you to stop calling me Doc."

Adam smart-assed back, "OK Doc."

Dr. Goodman snapped, "I really mean it. Don't call me Doc."

There was an enormous silence. Adam knew he hit some tender spot. Dr. Goodman never had spoken to him in that tone, or ever forbid him to say anything. That wasn't the understanding they had. Dr. Goodman's face was reddening and there was a slight tremor of his hand.

"I'm sorry Adam. There was something about your dream that hit some old cords in me."

Adam said, "You were a corpsman…they were the docs." He wasn't asking. He just knew. "You've been where I am." He felt a sense of relief, and hope.

Dr. Goodman smiled. "Isn't it uncanny? I was a combat medic in the army during World War II…now I know you were a Marine. The corpsman are the medics for the Marines." He paused. "You're right Adam. I've been where you are. Sometimes I get visits from the past. The scars are still there only not so red-hot sensitive." He waited. "So, you can't tell me about it yet?"

"This sounds crazy...I just realized we've been meeting once, sometimes twice a week for months and I haven't told you a goddamn thing about myself, not even that I was in the Marines. I'm sure you could tell, but I never actually said I was a Marine. Everything I told you was by describing my dreams." Both men were quiet. "Maybe next time. I'm sorry, really sorry I opened old wounds for you."

The next time they met Adam felt like a sixth-grader reciting in front of the class. His tone and cadence were flat and he felt outside of himself as he parroted,

"I'm Captain Adam Burns, UCMC, retired. Annapolis, 1949. Two tours in Korea, the first as a platoon leader and the second as a company commander. I have a jump wings, three purple hearts, a bronze and silver star. I have pins in my right femur that may come out some day and I'm missing part of my right lung. At the time of the wound to my leg and chest, I was rendered unconscious for a couple of weeks and I have no memory of what happened." He went silent. Drenched in sweat. They sat looking at each other for what seemed like a split second but turned out to be at least five minutes.

Dr. Goodman said, "Check your heart rate, Adam. I don't think you're connected up with yourself."

Adam's heart rate was better than 140. He had no feelings, barely remembering what he just said. It was as if he wasn't listening to himself and was split off into different compartments. Out of nowhere he started to sob. This time the dam broke and the tears flowed accompanied by a deep resounding bout of sobs that wracked every bone and muscle so that he had to hold his sides to still the pain. He couldn't stop until Dr. Goodman reached over and put his hand on his.

"Adam, this is part of what's been buried all these years. There's more to come but you're going to get through this."

That was when the real work began. Buried memories of every fire-fight, every man Adam lost, filled every hour. It was like a piece of him died with each of them, and there were too many "thems". Mostly kids, a few old timers in their thirties. The Koreans they killed and walked over like logs in the road, made a come-back. The No Names. A lot of No Names. His memories flooded the hours with facts, but the feelings were still buried. Horrendous and terrifying memories came across as flat recollections, as if he were telling a story about somebody else. Dr. Goodman's comments didn't help him get in touch with his feelings. One day Goodman caught himself dozing off. He was sure Adam noticed.

"Adam, you're putting me to sleep."

Adam rocked back in the chair, visibly hurt, and spat back, "That's your problem, Doc."

"No, it's our problem. You're telling me about being in combat, as if it happened to somebody else and

I'm getting sleepy because it feels to me like your not even in the room."

"You got a real problem, Doc. Maybe you need to see someone."

"I didn't mean to hurt your feelings Adam, but you're also pissed at me because it so painful to allow yourself to feel."

Adam got up — started for the door — Goodman beat him to it.

They stood there staring at each other. Goodman said, "I'll step out of the way if you really want to leave, but I wish you would stay. We don't have to talk, but you can't run away from your feelings without paying an awful price." He touched Adam's arm. "You've already paid too much...I know you'll be able to finally put this to rest."

It was a hard long road back to his chair. They were silent for the rest of the session, but when it was time to leave, Adam managed a smile and a whisper of thanks.

This session was a turning point for Adam. He realized that Goodman really cared when he put himself on the line and stood eye to eye with him. Shortly after, Adam started coming to therapy twice a week and at times asked for extra sessions.

Adam rode his bike up onto the sidewalk and parked next to Dr. Goodman's front door. He couldn't wait to tell him about Tom Exxes, so that's the first thing he did. He told him every detail, then waited for what he would say.

"Wow. The way you describe what happened I can almost smell this guy. I think you're right on. He was able to connect and trust you a bit because of how you reacted to him. You passed the test for now." He paused with his chin resting on the tips of his fingers as if he were meditating. "It's fascinating that you and Tom have similar ways of protecting yourselves." Before Adam could protest, he said, "Tom is psychotic and coats himself with his own shit to protect himself. Underneath he's terrified. You coat yourself with an invisible shield to protect yourself…underneath you're terrified."

"It may be fascinating to you but I don't feel terrified…I've been pretty open the last few weeks." Adam was starting to feel picked on and misunderstood. "Anyway, I want to use this session to get some help with Tom."

"Taking a look at what terrifies you will help your work with Tom."

"I don't see how I can take a look when I don't feel anything."

"That's what Tom would say, except he probably will start telling you about his family trying to kill him, and that's what's terrifying him."

Adam thought he may be right about Tom, but he couldn't see how that applied to himself. He fell silent, removed, and started to get angry. He stole a look at the clock hoping it was time to leave. "You're going to ask me why I was checking the clock."

"You beat me to it."

Adam mumbled under his breath, "Wise-ass prick."

"I missed the first part, but I think you called me a prick."

Adam started to laugh, "Wise-ass prick is what I said."

"Oh. Except you didn't say it. You mumbled and whispered it and now you're laughingly telling me what you called me. I think we're starting to get a handle on what you're so terrified about."

"And what's that, Doc?" Adam, was smiling and Goodman was dead serious.

"It's your anger and underneath there's a reservoir of rage…that's what terrifies you…you've been able to meld it into a charming up-front abrasiveness and sarcasm, but when you take the coating off it's a pile of rage."

Adam sat there speechless. Dr. Goodman didn't say anything. Adam knew he was talking about a part of him he didn't particularly care for, but he thought to say he was terrified was a bit of a stretch. He sat withdrawn into his own world and was startled to hear Dr. Goodman's voice.

"It's time to stop."

He left in a daze. Nearly wore himself out trying to kick-start his bike when he realized he hadn't
switched the ignition on. He sat there for about ten
minutes trying to collect himself. He thought of telling Dr. Goodman about how he felt just sitting there,
fantasizing him saying, "See — you're afraid of all that
power between your legs." That made him laugh as
he started his bike and gave the accelerator a twist or
two, hoping the roar of a 600 cc engine would give
Goodman a jolt.

His ride back to the hospital was one of those times
when all of a sudden you're where you wanted to be and
don't quite remember how you got there. One thing
for sure, whatever happened with Dr. G was filed away
somewhere. He was back to his cheerful charming self.
He unlocked the door to the ward and took one step
when he was greeted with,

"Good morning Dr. Burns. Thanks for being with
me last night. I hope you were able to get some sleep."
This familiar voice came from a neat man in hospital
pajamas. His tone and manner were formal and some-
what patronizing. Adam felt the sting in Tom's voice
and decided to put it on the back burner for the time
being.

"Tom. I didn't recognize you. You look great without all that shit smeared all over." Tom didn't seem
to react at all at being reminded of how he was when

they first encountered each other. Although he looked a hundred percent better cleaned up, he wasn't the spitting image of good health. His eyes were sunk into their sockets which made his head look too big for his long skinny neck to bear and left his ears to flap in the wind. He was emaciated. Not quite a holocaust victim, but he was getting there.

"My God Tom. When's the last time you ate? You look like you've been in a concentration camp."

"I couldn't eat. I didn't know if they poisoned my food. They held me down and stuck a tube through my nose into my stomach. They were trying to kill me. That's why I ran away."

He was sobbing uncontrollably. Adam tried to reach out to him but it was clear he didn't want to be touched. Adam decided to focus on the food.

"Hey Tom, what do you think we could do about finding food that's safe for you?"

The sobs stopped as quickly as they started. He laughed, with a hint of a maniacal twist to his mood. "You can be my taster." This was accompanied by a smart-ass grin, that reminded Adam, of a kid who just put something over on his teacher.

"That's a great idea and an easy solution, but what about when I'm not here? Maybe we can have designated tasters."

"You're not fucking with me, are you Dr. Burns?"

Adam was staring into a fierce intent face, and felt a chill run up his spine. This was a different voice coming out of this man. In an instant, Tom slipped from a stance of fear and desperation, to a short sniff of maniacal laughter, to the street-wise menacing tone with the posture to match.

"I'm not fucking with you Tom...you better not be fucking with me."

"Is that a threat Dr. Burns?"

"Yeah...It's a threat...I want a straight honest relationship with you...I expect you to level with me. Tasters are disposable people who taste food for the king. You're not the king and I'm not disposable. I'll taste your food first because I don't want you to starve to death, not because the food may be poisoned. We don't have people dropping like flies. I'm sure that most of the staff will be tasters if it helps you to eat because they're good people who care."

They stood, staring at each other. Adam didn't know what to expect next. Finally, Tom smiled and said,

"Thank you." He looked at Adam as if he were seeing him for the first time.

"May I call you Adam, Dr. Burns?"

"Sure, if I can call you Tom, Mr. Exxes."

He laughed. A genuine laugh. "You really are a ball buster, Adam."

Adam was tempted to say that it takes one to know one when the lunch tray arrived. He tasted everything on the tray and when Adam left the ward Tom was working on the dessert.

Adam didn't know it then, but that was the start of a relationship he would've never anticipated. Within a few minutes this man was delusional, depressed, maniacal and capable of a reasonably sane humorous duel of words. There was a combativeness in the air and Adam couldn't tell how much was emanating from Tom, or from himself. He knew Tom could make his spine tingle — a signal he couldn't ignore.

■■■

2

Adam managed to slip out of the psych pavilion without running into Vic. He wasn't up for a discussion about whether Tom was a paranoid schizophrenic, schizo-affective or a full blown hot manic-depressive, or being pushed to give up his last name.

It was the beginning of Spring, crispy, clear sky with the sun at its highest. He took the long way around the campus to the main hospital, taking in the sun as well as the engrossing way women walked. He loved to watch women walk. It didn't matter whether they were tall, short, fat or skinny. The variety of movement was captivating. He was tracking a nursing student who was making time down the path, almost at a run. She was heading into the sun and he could see her shape silhouetted against her white skirt, when the deafening noise of a chopper disrupted the relative calm. Adam froze as the adrenaline pumped a sense of vigilance in him and sent him into high alert, until he realized it was the Flight for Life copter coming into the pad next to the ER. He watched the flight team go into action.

It was a magnificent choreographed moment, a synchronized ballet with a cast who knew the steps, and the thumbs-up red-head was calling the cadence. It was the sight of her that released him from the spot he was glued to. His muscles were cramped and his heart felt like it was going to pop out of his chest. He had blips of troopers being loaded on copters. Within seconds the images were gone and he had no feelings. No anxiety, absolutely nothing. His feet were taking him to the ER and his head was focused on meeting the red-head, the rest would wait for his time with Dr. G.

The ER was erupting in orderly chaos. Victims from a multi-car collision were being triaged by a tall, well-endowed charge nurse. She was planted so no one could by-pass her scrutiny, directing traffic like a seasoned cop during rush hour. Adam stood admiring her moves and confidence when she glanced his way and said,

"Hey young psych doc, you still remember how to suture?"

Adam snapped back, "Sure. I also iron and do windows."

"You can help us out in room ten. It's the last one at the end of the hall. You know the way."

Room ten smelled like it had been sterilized since vacated by Tom. A young girl was lying on the table, arm extended with a clean four centimeter cut on her arm that had been cleansed and prepped for suturing. Her other arm was being comforted by her mom. A lovely picture compared to Tom. His new patient's name was Nancy who had no problem connecting. They started off with exchanging ages and it went on from there. By the time he put in eight fine sutures they were old friends. It was delightful. Adam felt like a real doc again and she was pleased with the relatively painless attention. He wondered, "What the hell am I doing in psychiatry?"

The sergeant at arms was back at the front desk, and the ER was down to a slow simmer. She broke a smile.

"Thanks for your help, and your help last night. You heard about the hug he gave me." She laughed, "I can still smell him."

Adam laughed, remembering Tom's description of her fat ass which looked pretty inviting to him. "He's unforgettable." He gave it a few seconds before asking, "Can you tell me the name of the red-headed doc who works here?"

"You mean Leslie Dillon." Her gaze went from his smiling face to his name tag. "Well, Adam, she's definitely not your type." He was reduced to an open mouth stare. "She's nice enough but tight-assed and going with a tight-ass cardiology resident who seems like a good fit. She's probably in the cafeteria, if you want to try your luck."

He noted her name tag and she was not the charge nurse but the doc in charge .

"Thanks, Dr. Silver."

"You can call me Lillian…if you don't score with Leslie I'll be here till three. I'm more your type." This was definitely not a seductive come on but more of a playful statement of fact. Adam was attracted to this no-nonsense, straight talking woman, and thought maybe he had met his match.

"I'll see you at three, Lillian."

He couldn't resist a stop in the cafeteria to check out the red-head. She was easy to spot in a blue flight suit and flaming red hair. She was sitting with a guy Adam thought might be her cardiology resident. It looked like he was reading a medical journal while she was staring into her drink. Adam picked up a coffee, walked over and introduced himself.

"Hi, I'm Adam Burns. I saw you in the ER last night and just watched you come off the helicopter. May I join you?" He completely ignored the guy who piped up with,

"We're having a private conversation."

Still looking at the red-head, he said, "Oh, sorry, it didn't look like you were together."

"We're at the same table, aren't we?"

"Yeah, but it didn't look to me like you were together." Adam, making a-to-do over reading her name tag, said, "If I were with lovely Leslie Dillon, I wouldn't have my nose in a medical journal."

His face turned red and he was about to sputter something when Leslie joined in with, "Walter and I are engaged, Dr. Burns."

"Oh damn...I was just about to ask you out." He looked at Walter and with faux-naif sincerity said, "I'm sorry Walter. My apologies. Congratulations." And to Leslie. "See you around, Dr. Dillon." He gave her his best smile. "You can call me Adam."

Adam thought, "The devil made me do that." He smiled, knowing he was being an arrogant asshole but he still enjoyed the encounter with this very proper uptight couple. Lillian was right on, Dr. Dillon wasn't his type. The rest of the afternoon was his. The only advantage of a night on-call. He finished his coffee, checked out with the ward and headed home.

Home was a one bedroom apartment in a newly renovated twelve story high rise owned by the University. It was well done with reasonable rents for graduate students, house staff and faculty. His digs were a bit bare. A queen size bed adorned the bedroom and a folding card table with a stool made up the dining area. There were seven oils and acrylics from unknown artists, whose work he just couldn't pass up, leaning against the wall. A ballerina in bronze held down the corner between adjacent windows.

With a pension and resident's salary he had plenty of money with no time to spend it. He could also count on at least a hundred every month from an on-going Poker game he lucked into during internship. He majored in Poker while recuperating at Bethesda Naval Hospital, and found a game of well healed docs who were the worst Poker players ever. He tries not to win too much too often so as not to wear out his welcome, but sometimes it's hard to do. The real story is, he has a shit-load of money sitting in a savings account, and every time he thinks about furnishing the apartment, he always finds something else to do. He knows there's something crazy about it, and for some unknown reason he has never brought it up in therapy.

He set the alarm for 2:15 and drifted off with thoughts of telling his shrink about his inhibition for buying furniture, and maybe his hand washing compulsion that he never mentioned in his therapy. They both quickly faded as fantasies of Lillian took front stage.

Adam felt like he had just closed his eyes when he found himself sitting bolt upright, his heart about to burst and in a pool of sweat. Lillian was nowhere to be found, only helicopters. He was dreaming that hundreds of helicopters were descending on him and he was paralyzed. Couldn't close his eyes, couldn't move a muscle. He managed to drag himself out of bed and make his way to the shower, where the dreams followed the soap down the drain. He was left with a vague memory of helicopters and a bit irritated about nothing in particular. He knew the buzz of irritation came with the dreams, but didn't know what to do about it except drink and he had enough of lost weekends.

Sitting still, by himself, wasn't his long suit. It's one of those times when he manufactured things to do as a distraction from living with himself. That's hard to do in a one bedroom apartment with a bed, folding card table and a stool. After mentally hanging the art he decided to transfer his bike from the hospital parking lot to the underground garage of his building, and then walk over to meet Lillian. That's one way to kill time and assuage the devils.

■ ■ ■

He was standing near the ER entrance talking with a police officer, while keeping an eye on the front desk where Lillian was giving her report. She had shed her scrubs for tan slacks, a black polo shirt with a sweater tied around her shoulders, almost exactly what Adam was wearing. She towered over the staff she was briefing, and her ass was curvy, inviting — everything but fat. Adam thought Tom was not only crazy but he didn't appreciate a beautiful ass when he saw one. As if to prove a point she bent over, retrieved her pack and made her way toward the door. She was strikingly attractive, not Hollywood gorgeous but authentically beautiful.

"Hi, Dr. Burns. I spotted you spying on me. Do you like what you see?"

They stood, eye to eye. Adam, was six-three. Lillian was close to six feet. Maybe a little over. He was thinking they were a good fit. There was something about this woman, that resonated with what was buried deep inside of Adam. It felt like they already met and this was a reuniting.

"Absolutely and ready for whatever the future holds."

"Well, Adam, what would you say for the immediate future, a walk over to the University athletic center for a swim. I usually swim to wind down after working a shift and you can get a better look at what the future may hold."

"I'll have to be a spectator. I haven't had time to join the center, and I don't have a bathing suit."

"That's easily remedied."

With no further elaboration she led the way to the athletic center, where Adam found, as a resident, he just had to sign up. Speedo swimsuits were for sale making any more excuses for not showing his body hard to come by. He slow-walked to the locker room and slipped on the briefest of brief swim suits made expressly for racers and serious swim types. Standing before a full length mirror he took stock of a strong body punctuated with enough scars to promote endless questions. Lillian couldn't have picked a better introduction to a part of his past that was still very much alive in the present. By dragging one begrudging foot after another he managed his way through the showers to the ten lane Olympic size pool. Lillian was already swimming laps so he slipped into the lane next to her and started off on a very slow freestyle.

He was surprised that he could use his right leg without pain. He did a lot of cycling but hadn't done any swimming since he got out of rehab, and that wasn't fun. After ten laps he rolled onto his back and fell into the relaxing cushion of water, from where he could contemplate the domed ceiling with all the suspended flags, large speakers and catch glimpses of Lillian as she slithered by showing no signs of slowing down. Adam was a good floater but he was getting water logged so he opted for a towel and a seat in the bleachers to cheer Lillian on. From that vantage point it was obvious she was a class act swimmer. He thought they could talk about her swimming rather than his scars.

When Lillian emerged from the pool it looked like she popped-out in one leap as if she were being propelled by some underwater spring. She waved and started into some serious stretching. She had his complete attention as well as his male member which started showing its appreciation. She was smiling as she walked toward him, unabashedly looking him over. Adam started to laugh and did a twirl on one foot showing off the back as well as the front.

She took her time and said, "Well it is my turn to look...I see we have a lot to talk about at dinner." She paused, her eyes traveling from the scar on the right side of his chest to the long scar down his right thigh and then to what was difficult to hide in a Speedo bathing suit. "That's an invitation."

"I'd love to have dinner with you." He managed to squelch what else he had in mind. It was too early to tell where this relationship would go. His track record in the arena of intimacy was nothing to write home about. Yet, he had a feeling about Lillian and so far liked what he felt.

They met at the front desk and decided to walk to a small Italian restaurant Lillian knew. It was about a mile along the river-walk and gave them time for those initial forays into unknown territories. Lillian wasted no time.

"Adam, what's with all those scars that adorn your beautiful body?"

For a moment he couldn't talk, but finally sputtered, "I don't know why it's so hard to talk about this...I think I want to tell you all about the scars...all about me...I wouldn't have gone swimming if I didn't, especially in a Speedo."

Lillian didn't say anything. Didn't try to reassure, coax or patronize him. She was serious and patient. Adam regained his voice.

"All the scars are from wounds I got in two tours in Korea. The smaller ones on my back were superficial wounds from shrapnel. A few months later I got nicked on my left arm. I was back on line in two weeks. The long scar on my thigh and chest was on the second tour. I don't have any memory of what happened. They tell me that it was a mortar hit. I was unconscious for a few weeks."

They walked some in silence and then Adam remembered the Flight for Life helicopter. "Something happened today which may have stirred some memories. I was walking toward the hospital when the Flight for Life chopper landed and I froze in my tracks. Couldn't move for a moment. Then this afternoon I took a nap and had a dream that was full of helicopters. I was told I was evacuated in a chopper. I was strapped in a stretcher to the pontoon and in the dream I was out in space. Maybe I'm getting some memory back."

He told Lillian he had a traumatic neurosis and was seeing Dr. Goodman. He stopped walking and turned toward Lillian, "So, do you still want to get to know me?" He was dead serious. He really wanted to know.

Lillian said, "This is good for starters. I've got a lot to tell you about me and then I'll ask you the same question." She smiled and took him by the hand. "Come on, let's eat. It will be my turn over dinner."

They sat at an outside table next to the river walk and split a very large delicious pizza. In between helpings of pizza and beer, Lillian talked and Adam listened. He loved the tone of her voice, her passionate energy in telling him about her family and her enthusiasm for living, which he envied. They had more in common than they imagined. Both grew up in Manhattan. Lillian on the Upper Eastside — Adam across the park on the Westside. Her parents are progressive reformed Jews who observe the main Jewish holidays.

They made sure Lillian and her younger sister went through all the rites of passage. She saw herself as a secular Jew and has no doubt as to who she is. When Adam told her his mother is Jewish and his father an Irish ex-catholic, Jewish convert, and an avowed atheist she said she sensed something familiar about him — it must be the Jewish half.

They were the only ones sitting outside, totally engrossed in each other so neither one noticed this dude coming up to their table wielding a baseball bat. He stood there, eyes glazed-over with a stupid frozen smile.

"Hey, big daddy, you got some green stuff you can spare?"

Adam was thinking how to take the bat and wrap it around his neck, when Lillian broke in.

"I have all our cash in my pack. Stay calm and I'll get it for you."

She was standing with her pack on the table, rummaging around for her wallet, while Mr. Dude stood drooling for what he expected to get. Lillian came up with a semi-automatic pistol, wracked a round into the chamber and said,

"If you move slowly and put that bat on the table I won't blow your balls off."

He got the no-choice command and Adam picked up the bat. The waitress stuck her head out the door and said they called the cops. The sirens could be heard off in the distance. Two cars showed up. One of the cops knew Lillian from the ER and told her to put her weapon on the table.

Lillian greeted the cop by name. "I've got a permit to carry. It's in my wallet in my pack."

It took about a half hour to tell the story to the cops during which the intruder started the shakes. Lillian suggested they make a stop at the ER to get this guy a fix before he came apart and vomited all over everyone. That speeded things up a bit.

Lillian looked at Adam, her eyes, cheeks and mouth crinkling up into a smile. "I told you I had a lot to tell you and now you know I carry a concealed weapon. I've also been a student of martial arts since I was fifteen. So do you still want to get to know me?"

"More than ever."

Adam was about to ask her what other surprises she had in store, when a man appearing to be in his late fifties came to the table with two enormous ice cream concoctions and introduced himself as Mario, the owner of Mario's. Dinner, dessert and double espressos came with the compliments of Mario.

Over espresso Adam said, "I suspect there's a story behind your carrying a gun and taking up the martial arts. Is that something you would want to tell me?"

"I don't know." She paused. "I'll give you the headlines, Adam, and if we move on in our relationship I'll tell you the whole story." The smile vanished along with any hint of playful banter. "I have two wounds to your three. You can't see the scars but they're there and still tender. I was raped when I was fifteen and then sexually assaulted five years later." She played with the ice cream, took a taste, to take a time out. Her eyes were misty, but there were no tears. She wasn't inviting any questions. "When I was fifteen I was swimming competitively and was being courted by several colleges. After the rape I quit swimming for a little more than a year and threw myself into weight strengthening and eventually into karate. I was out of school most of that year. I call it my year of empowerment." The dessert was turning to soup. "Five years later, towards the end of my sopho-more year, I was back swimming and getting ready for the Olympic try-outs, when I was assaulted in my dorm by a guy who wandered in off the streets. I managed to hold him off and someone must have heard me yell-ing and called the cops." She paused to work on her ice cream and espresso. "When I turned twenty-one I got some training in firearms then applied for a permit to carry. Today was the first time I ever used my gun…I'm glad he put the bat down."

"Yeah, so am I." Adam restrained himself from ask-ing what she would have done if he hadn't. He felt what she just told him was the tip of the iceberg and thought they both did well exchanging headlines. "Well Lillian, I think it's uncanny we found each other…I can't wait for the next chapter."

They started walking back along the riverfront. "I told you I was more your type." She retrieved that mischievous look. "I'd like it if you would walk me to my place. If you have ideas about making love with me, as I do about you, I want you to know it's not going to happen until we know each other better."

"Oh, damn. I was just about to say the same thing to you."

"No you weren't."

"No, I wasn't."

When they got to the medical center campus, Lillian said she only lived a few blocks from the hospital. Adam thought they both must live in the University apartments. It was as if she were inside his head.

"You probably have a place in the University apartments. I live two blocks north in the big high-rise." When they were in front of her building Adam, slowly, deliberately and softly kissed her on the lips and asked for her phone number. She kissed him back and asked for his.

■ ■ ■

The security guard opened the door for Lillian. Her knowing smile stamped her a witness to the good-night kiss. They both watched Adam wave and walk off.

"Just the first date, Jan. I'll keep you posted."

"I liked his looks from where I was standing."

Lillian laughed at the unsolicited critique. As the elevator door closed, she said,

"He looks even better close up."

Lillian lived in one of the two penthouse suites of this residential, commercial high-rise. A building a bit ahead of the times and owned by her family's investment corporation. She tapped in her code to open the door which silenced the security alarm. The suite was furnished in a simple, elegant contemporary style, bathed in subdued lighting with splashes of modern art, of her choosing.

She ejected the magazine and the round in the chamber of her Glock 26. She clipped the loose round back into the magazine, wondering how Adam really felt about her carrying a gun. He seemed pretty cool when she surprised their uninvited guest, but she thought most people would think she was off the deep end. When he told her of dreaming of helicopters coming after him, it reminded her of the dreams she has that wake her from a fitful sleep. She laughed, "Two traumatized nuts may make a compatible couple." She poured herself a vodka on the rocks and was about to check her messages when the phone rang. She listened to the recorder and when she heard her father's voice she picked up.

"Hi Dad. It's good to hear your voice."

"It's good to hear yours. I left you a couple of messages. I was beginning to worry about you."

"I love it when you worry about me. I just got in and was about to check my messages when you called...guess what...I wasn't working late, I was on a date."

"Oh, sweetie, that makes me so happy. Tell me about it."

"Well, it's a first date. He's one of the residents, but older, about my age. I met him in the ER...there was something about him that clicked for me. It's too early to tell, but I think he may be a keeper."

"That's wonderful. I don't think you've had a date in a couple of years, you really must be feeling better. Is it OK to share this with your mother?"

"Sure...you know I've been feeling better for the last couple of years, I just haven't met anyone I wanted to be with until I met Adam. After I got off work, I invited him for a swim. How's that for a first date? Then I invited him to have dinner with me. I've never done that before." She was excited and found herself sharing all she knew about Adam. "Maybe it's because he's been through a war, I was able to be open with him. I didn't tell him all I went through, but I know he understood what I felt. We just met, but I could sense some kind of bond. I hope I'm right about him."

Ben Silver, was tearing up as he listened to his daughter. He heard the life in her that had been dormant for far too long. He was reminded of what she had been through. The possibility of her being able to connect with someone she liked, was a welcome gift.

"Well, for starters I like his name. It's wonderful to share in your excitement. You've got to call your mother…keep me in the loop, but for now, I'm going to have to go. I have a meeting in an hour."

"Oh…where are you?"

"I'm in London. We're looking at some properties. Which reminds me to remind you there's a board meeting at the end of this month."

"I got it on my calendar. Dad, I love talking with you. Keep calling."

"I will. I love you."

Calls from her family always made her day, whether it was her mother, father or sister. She called them as often as they called her. They all suffered with her after she was raped. It was as if the whole family had been assaulted. She couldn't have asked for more support and caring, but in the end no one could completely erase the damage. Her therapist encouraged her to find ways to empower herself and as she became expert in the martial arts her confidence returned. She started to heal. She sent the second would-be rapist to the hospital on a stretcher.

Lillian finished her drink and was about to pour another vodka on the rocks when she felt she wouldn't need it to sleep through the night. She wondered if finding Adam enabled her to cancel the usual refill. Two stiff vodkas on the rocks usually allowed an uninterrupted sleep — but not always. Although it has been more than fifteen years since she was raped she still was plagued with flash backs and dreams of being raped and sodomized. At first the dreams were violent repetitions of the actual rape in which she was not only violated but her vagina and rectum were torn apart, leaving gaping holes. She would bolt awake in terror until she realized it was only a dream. Only a dream, only a dream, became her mantra to calm herself as she felt herself to be sure that it indeed it was only a dream. Over time the dreams started losing their intensity and the vodka helped. Often times she would be dreaming and part of the dream would be her own reassuring voice saying, it was only a dream.

The rape left its mark on the way she thought about herself. Although she knew better, deep down she felt damaged and unlovable. She found ways to titrate the amounts of closeness that she could allow with both the men and women in her life. The only sexual pleasure she had was what she provided herself and she couldn't share her sexual fantasies with anyone, even her therapist.

Lillian poured the second vodka, as she wondered what it was about Adam that drew her to him. There was something about his face, the scar over his right eye and the way he spoke that signaled something reassuring to her. She had never been that forward with a man before. She felt a certain kinship with him when she saw his scars.

After a hot bath she would soon see what the night had in store.

■ ■ ■

Adam slept through the night. If he had dreams there were no remnants of them when he awoke, but his right hand was stiff as if he slept with a clenched fist. Clenched fists and cramping muscles were the usual accompaniments of his horror dreams. By the time he hit the shower all he could think of was Lillian. He loved her being so up front and comfortable about his scars. He had never been with any woman quite like her, or any man for that matter. He was laughing out loud when he thought of her pulling the 9mm out of her pack and seeing the look on the guy's face was priceless. As he was getting dressed any joy was over-taken by the cloud that usually hung near by. He thought, there was no one in his life that he could talk to and share what happened yesterday except Dr. G. He had no close friends. The men he was close to in the service were either dead or living all over the states or world. He kept track of a few who were still on active duty and with old dear friends from early on, but he hadn't seen or talked with any for at least a year. Most of his friendships in med school were with women he was involved with, who he was unable to stay connected to for very long. He was off and running at any sign of a deepening intimacy and he didn't want that to happen with Lillian. He didn't want to be the cause of anymore hurt for her. She already had her lifetime quota.

Adam walked over to the hospital hoping to meet Lillian in the cafeteria. He had to settle for his residency group. They were all four or five years younger. He felt like an older brother and sometimes sibs get on each others nerves. Vic, the chief resident, was particularly annoying to Adam, especially when he flashed those empathic eyes that claim to know exactly how you feel.

They were talking about a paper they were supposed to read for a class. They were dissecting it, letting all the juice run out. Adam was able to focus on his eggs and overdone bacon, which allowed him to listen and to curb his impulsive nature. He liked his colleagues-in-training, but in this group of five he didn't think any of them knew how to walk the gutters, sample the sewerage and learn from the smell. He was a snob and could be overbearing when it came to knowing the street. He was too rough around the edges to fit the empathic psychiatrist model.

When they finished the paper dissection and breakfast they moved to the psych pavilion for morning rounds. Brenda Dobbs, the on-call resident, described what sounded like a busy night in the ER. Brenda looked like she hadn't gotten to sleep, but she always looked sleep deprived. She's one of those intense types who look you right in the eye, listening so intently you start to think what you are saying is important enough to shape world events, until you realize she listens to everyone in exactly the same way. She's an attractive woman, who presents herself with an apology for being and hides the fact she has curves. Brenda had attached herself to Adam in the early anxious month of the residency, until she felt more settled, but she still tended to talk to him, as if the group wasn't there. It made Adam uncomfortable and he thought she really needed a mature nurturing woman to help her blossom into womanhood. He didn't think a man could do that for her. She was in the midst of describing a sixteen year old girl in DT's when the phone rang. Vic picked-up and said,

"Adam, you need to get to the ward. Tom is acting up and screaming for you."

Vic's tone sent Adam off on the run. No one calls unless they really have to. When he got to the ward Tom was backed into a room holding one of the nursing aides with one arm stretched over her shoulder and around her chest, while the other hand held a fork to her carotid artery. She was terrified. Tom started to smile when he saw Adam. Before Tom could get a word out, Adam said,

"Tom, is this anyway to behave in a hospital?" He didn't know why he said it but it was the first thing that came to his mind. He could see Tom thinking about it, when he said,

"She has a crooked vagina."

Adam stepped out of his understanding mode and adopted the tone he heard coming out of Tom. "If you don't let her go I'm going to give you a crooked prick after I knock you on your ass."

Tom started to laugh. That maniacal laugh. He let the poor woman go and dropped the fork. He could hardly stop laughing when he said, "Adam, you sure have a way with words."

"Words...bullshit...we need to talk."

He meekly followed Adam down to the therapy room. Tom paused at the nurse's station and apologized to the aide.

"I'm really sorry. I lost it when you told me you tasted the pudding and I knew you hadn't. What I did was crazy, but that's why I'm here." He started to laugh again and stopped himself. "Sorry."

Adam sat in the chair nearest the door. In case Tom wasn't able to control himself, he wanted a quick exit to get help. He was in a quandary of what to do next, when Tom flashed a full-tooth smile and said,

"You're thinking, what am I going to do with this nut?"

"You're right on, Tom. I'm also thinking that I need to stay connected to the sane part of you so both of us can understand the crazy part." Adam waited. When Tom didn't respond he said, "So the woman with the crooked vagina, meant that the woman was crooked. She lied to you."

He started to go off on his laugh but caught himself. "Pretty neat, huh?"

"Yeah it is, but it's also pretty crazy." Adam waited. "Tom, when I talk to your sane self you seem to come to your senses."

"That's because you mean what you say. I know your penis is not crooked." He started to laugh again. "I can't seem to stop it, can I? It's scary when these thoughts just pop out...what's scarier is when I think my head is going to explode with thoughts and words I can't turn off. That's when I think about killing myself...that scares me because I may not be able to stop."

"Tom, how much do you know about manic-depressive illness?"

"I know it runs in families, it sure does in mine. The latest thinking is there's a genetic predisposition, it's mainly a chemical imbalance...that's how it feels to me. I also heard about a new treatment, Lithium, that may control the mood swings and crazy thinking."

"If you know all this why haven't you tried Lithium?"

"Well, at the last place I was they were arguing about whether to shock me or to start Lithium. They never asked me what I thought. They talked about all this as if I wasn't in the room. I didn't trust them.

I thought they were trying to kill me...I ran away. Maybe because my brother was my legal guardian and I don't trust him."

"Tell me about your brother."

"I really don't want to talk about him." He zipped his mouth closed and sat with his hands folded, trying to look serious. He looked like a little boy playing the game of who was going to smile first.

Adam said, "Fair enough. Let me tell you what's going on in my head and you tell me if what I think fits you."

Tom said, "Fair enough." Then broke out with his maniacal laugh. When he was able to gain control he said, "I'm sorry I mocked you. I just can't stop it and not being able to control myself drives me crazy." He smiled. "You must admit that you can't screw someone with a crooked vagina unless you have a crooked penis."

Adam let that one pass. "Tom, what comes out of your mouth makes you laugh, makes me laugh too, but I know it's not so funny when you can't control it. There's also a lot of anger in your mocking and mimicking." Tom nodded. He had that so-what-else is new look. His condescending smirk was putting Adam off, creating a distance between them. Adam said, "I think you get scared when you feel I'm getting too close...you push me away with your sarcasm to protect yourself...if that doesn't work you'll smear yourself with feces."

Tom jumped out of the chair blurting out, "I'm not going to suck your cock, Adam."

"I'm not going to suck your cock either, Tom." Tom retreated to the corner and looked as if he was about to bolt for the door. Adam scooted his chair back to give Tom a clear shot at the door if he had to leave. He went on talking to whatever healthy part of Tom he could reach and he was reaching when he said, "That's what your brother did, make you suck his cock?"

Tom had resumed that little boy look with posture to match. "And now he wants me dead. He doesn't want anyone to know what we did."

There was a silence that seemed to last forever. They just looked at each other. Adam was exhausted. He really didn't know what else to say. He changed the focus to see if Tom could talk about more neutral things about his family. Tom was still guarded about revealing much about his family, but did say he had a sister who is fifteen years older and his brother was ten years older.

"I don't think they wanted anymore kids. I was the change of life kid when I popped on the scene." Tom started to laugh, pointing his finger as if he was firing a gun. "Pop, pop, pop....." Adam interrupted him on the sixth pop.

"Tom, what would you think about our looking into whether Lithium could help with your thinking and the sudden swings in mood. The part that makes you so crazy and drives you nuts."

"I'd be willing to look into it. Would you taste it first?" The contagious laugh filled the room. Adam couldn't help but laugh with him.

Adam said, "I'll think about it, but maybe you'll have to be the taster."

When he left Tom, his head was spinning. He had never spent such an intense hour with anyone who had split second mood swings and whose thinking could fluctuate so rapidly. One second he sounded completely rational and the next as crazy as a loon. Adam knew he needed to bring himself to consult with Vic. He wasn't particularly enthused about that . On the other-hand he couldn't wait to tell Dr. G about Lillian.

■■■

6

Adam thought if he were going to keep up with Lillian, he'd better start getting in shape. He had a fairly new 10-speed bicycle, and there was a dedicated bike path most of the way to Dr. G's office. Once he got the tires pumped up, the idea of moving himself by his own power without the noise of 600cc's felt pretty good. There were no traffic jams on the bike path, in fact he made better time than he did on his motorcycle.

As usual, Dr. G was right on time. Adam wanted to talk to him so badly he couldn't wait and now that he was with him he didn't know what to say or where to begin. So that's what he said. "I couldn't wait to see you…now I don't know what to say or where to begin."

"Take your time Adam. Let it all settle down and it will be easier for you."

Adam didn't think he needed help with managing his insides but evidently he did. He let it settle, it was easier. He started talking about Lillian, non-stop, pausing for air. He hadn't realized how excited he was about her until he started talking. He also realized how starved he was to have someone to talk to. Goodman listened with an obvious smile of pleasure.

"Adam, I'm happy for you. I've never seen you this happy for yourself."

"It's a bit uncanny that I met someone whose been traumatized. I think there must be some unconscious attraction."

"It's a good bet. What sort of trauma did Lillian have?"

Adam told him about her being raped when she was fifteen, her competitive swimming and her being assaulted when a sophomore in college. When he told him about the incident at the restaurant and Lillian carrying a concealed weapon, Adam could see the concerned look on his face.

"Don't worry, I don't think she's a loose cannon with a loose cannon...she's empowered herself through martial arts and carrying a gun. Maybe a little over the top, but she's not ever going to be a victim again." He waited for Goodman to say something.

"Weren't you surprised when she fished a gun from her pack?"

"You know it's funny. I was sizing this guy up, thinking how to take the baseball bat from him when I heard her say she had all our cash in her pack. I was wondering what she was up to, then she came up with a semi-automatic pistol. The expression on the guy's face changed….I felt like I was watching a movie. You know…sort of there but not really there…just watching all this happening." Goodman was quiet and Adam wasn't up for a prolonged silence. "You think she's a little nuts about protecting herself?"

"Not nuts. Maybe a bit over the top, as you said. What do you think she would have done if he didn't put the bat down?"

"I think if he started to attack with the bat she might have shot him to disable him. I'll ask her. I would have blown him away. At least I think I would have. If you have a gun it's an easy next step to use it. What would you have done?"

"I don't know. I don't carry a concealed weapon, but then I've never been raped. I can only imagine how horrible that would be." He sat. Pensive. His chin resting on his finger tips. A familiar pose. "You thought that people who have experienced trauma may somehow attract one another. I was thinking that here are three of us who have experienced life threatening events, who have ended up as doctors. The healing profession. I don't see guns in that picture. It must have been awful for Lillian. She must still feel so very vulnerable. Maybe that makes carrying a gun more understandable." They both were quiet.

"I know the time is up but I wanted to tell you one of the things I realized since we last met. It's how alone I've been.......how much I love being able to meet with you." He took a deep breath. "How much I love you." He couldn't believe what was coming out of his mouth.

"I know Adam. I love you too."

Adam responded, "Even though I would have blown the guy away?"

Goodman smiled, "I think I just made you very uncomfortable."

Adam was blushing when he left. Uncomfortable, was an under-statement. He never said that to another man, even his father. He never told a woman he loved her either. He thought he must have told his mother that he loved her when he was little, but had no memory of it. He had a rush of loosely connected thoughts about how he loved his mother and father, and needed to tell them both that he loved them. He hadn't ever thought about how hard it was for him to say, I love you. It doesn't come easy.

"I wonder if Dr. G tells all his patients that he loves them. I'm going to ask him. I'm going to ask him if he's gay...if he thinks I am. I don't think he could bring himself to blow the guy away. I'm going to ask him about that also." He was laughing out loud, when a passer-by flashed him an, "Are you crazy" look. He realized that he was sitting on his bike broadcasting all this dribble and hadn't moved an inch. He thought, "Maybe I don't want to leave Dr. G. Maybe I'm going to drive myself nuts."

Cycling back to the hospital he noticed a stretched feeling in his right thigh. He thought he was overdue for a checkup on his leg, as well as a pulmonary function evaluation. Then he wondered why he was concerned about his body all of a sudden. He thought it's the curse of being in psychiatry. Always under the magnifying glass.

———

Adam grabbed a sandwich, made rounds on the ward, then gave in to the burning desire to see Lillian. He took a quick detour to the ER to catch a glimpse of her as she flashed by. The ER was in action mode and he wasn't up to being conscripted to the suture squad again, although part of him envied the action. He left a note asking her to dinner and made a quick exit.

He made a stop at the medical library to do a search for what he could find on Lithium. After making copies of the newest articles, he headed back to the psych pavilion. He was happy to see Tom asleep, since he hadn't ordered any sleep meds. He had hoped Tom would be able to turn his motor off without them, as he didn't particularly want to go through the tasting routine again. He left the articles for Tom along with a note that he would see him tomorrow.

Adam reluctantly sought out Vic, who was a walking resource on every psychopharmacological agent that has ever been invented. Vic was delighted to be sought out. When Adam described Tom's symptoms, Vic thought Lithium might be of help to him. The clinical trials on treating manic-depression with Lithium were promising. Vic wanted to see Tom and mentioned that the attending psychiatrist was pushing to find out Tom's real name. Adam managed to restrain himself and told Vic he needed more time, but maybe they could test things out tomorrow when they saw him.

There was a message from Lillian waiting in Adam's mailbox. She thought she would be a little late but would love to meet around four. Would he be up for a swim and then dinner? He was already up for it. He would have time to pick up his new Speedo, a small day pack with some stuff to make him smell his best and still make a class on psychopathology.

■ ■ ■

7

At four, Lillian was still in scrubs giving a report to her replacement. A cap and mask testified to a busy day and the spatter on her shoes to a bloody one as well. She gave Adam a smile of recognition and two fingers signaled a short wait, so he parked himself at a spot where he had a good view of this new woman in his life. The sight of her filled him with warmth and he wondered if he was falling in love with this intriguing woman who he hardly knew. He watched her move with grace and confidence, and saw how she was listened to. He liked what he saw.

Lillian, relieved of command, walked over and took Adam's hand. "Sorry to keep you waiting. It's been one of those days. Come to the lounge while I change."

Adam followed her to the staff lounge and watched as she slipped out of her scrubs, threw everything including her canvas shoes in a bag, marked with her name and jump shot it all into a laundry bin. She was into her khakis and black tee in a time that defied the stereotype of how long it took women to get ready. They headed for the old swim hole.

"I loved watching you give the report. It was a treat seeing you change. You made my day."

"I'm happy I'm pleasing to you. You turn me on too." She smiled. "With your pack on we look like twins. Are you packin?"

"No…are you still carrying?"

"I'm always carrying. How does that sit with you?"

"It really worries me. If you're carrying and you point a weapon, you need to be prepared to use it. I've seen guys who have hesitated and are not around to tell about it. It may create more trouble than it solves."

"Well, you're right but it makes me feel empowered. Not safer, just empowered…in charge."

"I know, but what would you have done if he came after you with the bat? I think I could have disarmed him without a gun and my guess is that you could also,."

"You're probably right. Maybe that's the best argument for not carrying." She led Adam to a bench outside the Athletic Center. "If he attacked us with the bat I would have squeezed off several rounds and he would be gone." She took a breath. "The guy who assaulted me in my dorm room was carried out on a stretcher. At his trial he kept looking at me with that 'wait till I get out bitch look'. I kept thinking I should have finished him off. Then I wouldn't have to worry about his getting out and getting even. It's been twelve years...he probably will get paroled soon." She fell silent and turned to face Adam head on, " So my new friend, do you still want to get to know me?"

"If I had the gun and he attacked I would've blown him away. If I didn't have the gun I couldn't have blown him away." He searched for a clue to what she was thinking. "So, do you still want to get to know me?"

"Let's swim."

Adam took his time getting out to the pool. He was letting the last words sink in, thinking about how easily they had been talking about taking a life. He didn't like that part of himself. He wondered about her.

He wandered out to the pool and sat on the diving platform watching Lillian in her element. She was into a butterfly with an incredibly smooth dolphin kick. She did four laps before rolling into a backstroke without missing a beat. Adam slipped into the water, into a slow free style getting propelled by strong arms with a weak kick. He watched Lillian slither by as he took a breath trying to beef up his kick, then started laughing at his futile attempt to compete. After twelve laps, two more than the day before, he collapsed into a float to the ladder, then to the bleachers. Lillian was in a last lap of breaststroke and after the turn came up into freestyle. He counted fourteen more laps before she popped out of the pool into her stretches. As he watched her move into the different postures, for some reason his erotic dial was turned down, not even a twitch.

She came to him smiling. "Ready for dinner? I know of a quiet place where we can be safe." All the life and death issues defused in humor.

She took him to a quiet place where they ate and talked about everything except guns and killing, each afraid of losing the connection they both desperately wanted. After dinner they walked along the riverfront back to the park near the hospital campus. Lillian shared her excitement over the plans for establishing a specialty in emergency medicine. Adam told her about Tom and how draining it was trying to keep up with his racing thoughts and mood swings, the crooked vaginas and penises. He heard himself saying that he loved being in Maurice Martin's Department of Psychiatry, a man he admired, but he wasn't sure he wanted to be a psychiatrist. It was the first time he said that out loud, maybe the first time he allowed himself to even seriously think it. He was beginning to realize that he found a safe-house in the Department of Psychiatry. He wasn't sure he wanted it as a permanent residence. It was a good holding station.

"Hey Lillian, how about holding?"

"Holding?"

"Yeah, holding each other." He felt giggly, maybe a bit maniacal like Tom. "I'm formally proposing we hold each other. I would love to hold you."

"Your serious?" *You're*

"Absolutely serious. I would love you to hold me...if you would like to."

"I'd like that. I wish I'd thought of it. Where shall we hold each other?" She laughed. "I meant where shall we go?"

"My place. I have a brand new bed and a very old card table."

So Lillian got her first look at his digs. The bed, the very old card table and a stool seated next to it.

"I plan to shop for furniture this weekend. If you're free and want to help, I can sure use it."

"Well Adam, I think your place has great possibilities...I'd love to help."

They stood looking and slowly undressing each other. Lillian felt every scar on his body, gently, as if they could be smoothed out by her touch. Adam softly felt her breasts, her nipples hard, her body smooth and firm.

"Adam, I think we have a straight penis intruding."

"Just ignore him. He has a mind of his own. He may not fall asleep when we do."

"Adam, I'm not ready to have you in me."

"I know. We're holding each other." He stroked her back, she smoothed his scars. The straight penis went its own way. They slept. No dreams.

When the alarm battered the soft silence of sleep, he was spooned into Lillian and she was not ready to release her catch. He turned, kissed her and said, "I hope you slept as well as I did. I wouldn't mind making a habit out of sleeping with you."

"It was the most restful sleep I've had in years. It usually takes two vodkas on the rocks. Sometimes three. It felt good to be held and to hold you. Glad I thought of it."

They moved to the shower and eventually out the door reluctantly parting until four, when they would start over.

■ ■ ■

He was whistling on his way to the psych pavilion, and must have been smiling judging from all the smiles he got from people he passed. He wasn't used to feeling so good. He always had an ear out for the shoe to drop. At morning rounds people picked up on his elated mood — one thought that he either just inherited a shit load of money or got laid. They didn't believe him when he told them he was finally able to get a good nights sleep. Brenda gave him the intense look — he thought he was about to get an insightful empathic comment. She smiled a knowing smile — he smiled back. Vic came in with some Danish, then Steve Greenberg shared his horrendous night on call.

"I'm glad you slept well…as soon as I'm finished telling you how I spent the night I'm heading for bed." He told of his encounter with the first case of full blown DTs he had ever seen. "The guy was terrified, wiping spiders he thought were crawling in every orifice and bugs coming out of the walls. We no sooner had him stabilized and admitted to medicine than a another guy presented with alcoholic halucinosis."

Vic ran through the possible treatment of both these patients, then Steve went on about a woman with suicidal thoughts and an older man who just lost his wife of 55 years. Everyone was getting fidgety. Bob Hansen and Eric Foster, the other two residents in the group, started cracking wise. Vic brought us all back to a reasonable state with a comment about how the Psych ER can be anxiety producing. It was an intellectual comment that understated what everyone was feeling but it helped. Sort of a release valve. Adam was beginning to admire Vic.

After rounds Adam prepared Vic for the encounter with Tom. He told him, "You don't just meet with Tom. You come away feeling like you just went a round or two and have been smeared, if not actually with feces, its psychological equivalent."

"I'm looking forward to meeting him. He sounds like a real challenge."

Tom was waiting for them at the door to his room.

"Hi Tom. How are you this morning?"

"I am wonderful, Adam. And how are you this morning?" He started his laugh as he mimicked Adam's voice and gestures. "I'm losing my fucking mind, Adam. That's how I am, I'm in a jam, and I don't like the jelly they serve, it sits in my belly and doesn't move a damn." He gave Adam a wink. "So that's how I am."

"Tom, I asked my Chief Resident to help us decide about Lithium. Is that OK with you?"

"It's OK with me if it's OK with you. I'll meet the Chief, but if he's a thief the meeting will be brief." The maniacal laugh burst forth and instantly faded into sobs. "I'm clanging and I need a banging." He started to bang his head on the wall. Adam grabbed him and held him and to his surprise Tom collapsed in his arms. "Thank you Adam. I'm not going to suck your cock."

Adam waited till he collected himself. "Are you ready to meet my Chief Resident? His name is Vic Fuerte."

Tom nodded and called out, "You can come in now, Dr. Fuerte. You've had one ear in anyway, haven't you?"

Adam was waiting for him to take off on Vic's name, but he was as normal as can be. He shook hands with Vic and turned toward Adam. "I bet you thought I'd be rhyming Vic, with you know what." He suppressed the laugh with a quick zip of his lips.

Vic said, "May I call you Tom?"

"Sure, may I call you Victor?"

"You can call me Vic, but I would prefer Dr. Fuerte."

"Fair enough…oh really not a level field…I can not yield to Vic the chief…but Vic has a straight dick…he doesn't sound like a thief but we're going to be brief."

Vic waited for Tom to take a breather, when he saw that wasn't going to happen he broke through the chatter. "Tom, we need to do a thorough evaluation and I need you to cooperate." It was Vic's no nonsense tone that enabled Tom to descend from the clouds and participate in a mental status and physical exam. Adam was amazed that he allowed Vic to examine him. Tom remained cool and collected, answering questions, doing calculations and showing no fear of being touched. He did tell Vic there would be no rectal exam and he recited a rhyme about Vic not touching his dick that made them all laugh. Then Vic asked about Tom's background and family. Tom told him he didn't want to talk about his family. When Vic persisted, Tom zipped his mouth closed and fell silent. End of conversation.

Then there was a serious discussion about Lithium. Tom had read the articles Adam left for him and had some good questions which Vic answered, including that he didn't know why or how Lithium worked. He told Tom Lithium used for manic-depression was a recent discovery. Tom agreed to give it a try. He agreed to having blood drawn and to have x-rays of his head and lungs. There was no sign of paranoia. He appeared to be more trustful and less frightened. When Vic left, Adam decided to take advantage of Tom's stable state.

"Tom, it seemed like you felt it was safe to talk with Vic."

"I can tell Vic is an honest person and genuinely wants to help me, like you do. He's an uptight guy though, but he'll mellow as he gets older. I can see you hadn't told him who I am. I didn't think you would. You've been around, Adam, and you're not easily intimidated."

Tom rambled on about Adam. It was uncanny how right on the mark he was. He knew Adam had experiences he didn't want to talk or think about. Adam half-thought Tom might be clairvoyant and knew about his tours in Korea. When Tom finally ran out of gas Adam asked,

"Tom, why is it so important for you to know so much about me?"

"It's crucial, not just important. I'm falling in love with you...I don't want to suck your cock."

"You mean you don't want me to exploit you?"

"No goddamn it. I don't want to suck your cock. What's the matter with you? You have shit in your ears? You don't get it. Two fucking years and no one gets it." He ranted, raved, raged, clanged and Adam thought he was about to start banging when he suddenly stopped and started to shake uncontrollably. At first Adam thought he was having a seizure but it was more of a violent shiver. He tried to put a blanket around him.

Tom shouted at the top of his lungs, "Get the fuck away from me," which drew a nurse and aide to the door. It looked like it was about to escalate into a wild, violent melee. Adam motioned them away—it suddenly hit him that somehow he had set this whole thing off. Tom sat holding himself—shivering, teeth chattering as if he was perched on a cake of ice. Adam sat quietly thinking over what he had said or done to precipitate Tom's reaction. He finally decided to say what he felt.

"Tom, I'm very sorry I made you feel so bad." He put the brakes on, left it at that and waited. The shivering morphed into spasms. Tom took a long searching look at Adam. It took a few minutes for Adam to connect Tom's forlorn sad look to what might have happened to set off his rage. Adam said,

"When I didn't understand you, I could have just as well not been here. You must've felt like I left you out in the cold."

Tom sat there in silence, tears starting to roll, no words to match. The spasms stopped. Adam didn't know how accurate he was, but knew he reconnected with Tom. He didn't know what else to say. The only thing he knew was, he needed to be there. So he waited. It seemed like a very long time Tom sat looking at Adam, unblinking, the tears leaving dry rivulets on his sunken cheeks. He started to say something, stopped and then said,

"I felt I was exploding and would hurt you. I'm glad you stayed with me."

Adam started to tear up and Tom handed him a tissue. When he hesitated taking it Tom smiled, "There are no rules prohibiting patients from caring for their doctors."

Adam left feeling in over his head. He was amazed at this sensitive, empathic, crazy nut who one minute was losing it and the next was looking after him. He looked for Vic, who was nowhere to be found and ended up in the lounge with a cup of old coffee thinking about Tom.

He went over every detail he could remember. Tom flew into a rage when Adam didn't understand what he meant when he said he was falling in love and didn't want to suck his cock. But it wasn't just rage. Tom was actually shivering as if the temperature had dropped to below zero. Adam was wearing himself out, decided to give it a rest and fell asleep holding a half full cup of coffee.

He didn't know how long he was asleep when he felt someone unfolding his grip on the coffee cup. It was Vic, who didn't know how close he came to getting laid out.

"Sorry to startle you, Adam. I thought you were going to spill the coffee all over you."

"Thanks Vic, I'm glad you woke me. I wanted to get your take on something that happened with Tom."

Vic listened, tilting his chair back, eyes half shut, as if he was letting it all flow through his unconscious, anticipating a hit, a connection that would bring instant meaning to Tom's eruption. When Adam finished — he waited — and waited— finally Vic came through with a comment that at first seemed not worth the wait.

"Adam, I think you're right. It was your not understanding him that set Tom off. It does sound like he felt abandoned, cut off, his shivering elicited your remark about leaving him out in the cold. We can come up with lots of ideas of what he means when he says he loves you, but doesn't want to suck your cock...all the ideas may turn out to be dead wrong. You were able to reconnect with him...I think he'll eventually tell you, either in words or action, what being with you means. At this point, I think you're treating the crooked penises, the vaginas, and his cock sucking talk, as his special language, helps him to not feel so alone in his misery. That's what he needs now."

Adam was totally surprised how Vic was able to objectify what happened between he and Tom, in a way that brought some order to the chaos he was feeling. Vic was coming up in Adam's book. "Thanks Vic. You've been very helpful."

Adam left thinking that he had been too hard on Vic — he needed to ease up on the sarcasm at rounds and not be such an asshole with people. He thought, "Maybe I'm getting better — maybe my work with Dr. G is helping — maybe falling in love." Without much thought he was walking toward the cafeteria. He took the long way around the campus, taking in whatever was in bloom including the young students who blossomed throughout the seasons, giving himself some alone time.

It was hard to botch a breakfast or lunch so the cafeteria was near full, compared to dinner time when you can almost eat in private. He saw Lillian who was sitting with the beautiful red-head but after he loaded up on turkey salad, fruit bowl and ice tea he was hesitant to join them. He hoped Lillian would look up and welcome him with open arms, and as if she could read his thoughts she looked his way, smiled and beckoned him to her. Adam thought she must have caught his scent.

"Adam, come join us. This is Leslie Dillon," and to Leslie, "This is Adam Burns."

In chorus they both said, "We've met," then laughed — then simultaneously started to tell how — then each deferred to the other — then Lillian stepped in designating Leslie as the starter. Adam discovered Leslie, while not exactly a free spirit, wasn't as up-tight as when she was with Walter. He managed to refrain from tweaking her every time she went rigid as he watched Lillian deftly help her to loosen up. Leslie finished her lunch and excused herself. She sounded a bit like a child asking if she could leave the table to go play.

"Well you were right, she is up-tight…she sure as hell defers to you."

"She's respectful of her superiors and I'm her boss. She knows emergency medicine, but I had to tell her she couldn't proselytize in the ER. I'm not sure I got through to her but if she does it again I'm going to fire her ass. Today was the second warning. I'm her boss in the ER but I think she answers to a higher boss."

Adam was dying to know what got to Lillian and all it took was a quizzical look.

"Leslie is part of a Christian fundamentalist group. I can put up with her 'God blessing' everyone and everything but I won't tolerate her telling a teenager who's asking for contraceptive advice to just say no, and then not referring her to the adolescent clinic or her telling a woman enquiring about terminating her pregnancy that she ought to reconsider before murdering her baby."

"This isn't what you were talking about when you invited me to join you?"

"No. It was at least an hour before and it was pretty heated on my part. She sat in my office with a supercilious smirk, like she forgave me for I knew not what I was doing. She thanked me, God blessed me, then showed up at my table as if nothing happened." Lillian took a bite of her sandwich. "It makes me wonder if I actually did tell her if she didn't follow procedure I'd fire her." The sandwich got the brunt of her anger.

Adam had a poignant thought about what Leslie needed and he was sure he could find some scripture to give it currency.

"Adam, I know what your thinking and it wouldn't help her a bit."

"How in the world did you know what I was thinking?"

"You had this clever little smile on your face. I thought you had suddenly come up with everyman's solution for uptight women." She gave her sandwich a reprieve. "I don't think she's uptight in the sense that you do. She's unbending in her beliefs and thinks she's doing God's bidding. She's a passionate soul and spreads God's word on everything and everyone she touches, and she pisses me off."

Adam was thinking Lillian ought to go into psychiatry and he should be the ER doc. He was aroused by her fire and wanted to move past the holding, as much as he liked being held. He wanted to know her, everything about her and did want to be inside her. He never felt this way about anyone before. He wasn't sure what this way was all about, but it felt alive. He felt alive for the first time in years.

They finished lunch and when Adam asked Lillian if she would like to swim and dine together, she smiled,

"You know this is Friday, we could spend the whole weekend together."

Adam didn't need any coaxing. He was pleased Lillian was willing to put herself out there. He had the same thought but was afraid to ask. He was beginning to realize how fragile he felt beneath his protective armor. When he left Lillian he felt at loose ends. He didn't know what to do with himself — where to go — at a loss. The image of Tom came thundering back in spades. He tried to imagine his own feelings under a psychotic lens — magnified by the power of ten or a thousand. He would be coming apart at the seams, flying into a rage, exploding with no restraint, no modifiers. That's what happened with Tom, or at least something like that.

He was excited as he walked back to the Psych Pavilion. He discovered something new. He also realized he wasn't at loose ends. He regained his focus and was reconnected with himself. For some reason Tom couldn't do this on his own. Adam was all pumped up and wanted to find Vic to tell him of his discovery.

Vic was in his office totally engrossed in inspecting a small black box.

"Hi Adam, come in. We have these new pagers for everyone." He handed one to Adam and spent the next five minutes telling him about this new technology. Adam wasn't happy about being on an electronic leash and didn't want to get into a discussion about pagers. He signed for his, clipped it to his belt and decided he didn't want to tell Vic about his new discovery. He started to leave when Vic said,

"Hey Adam, you wanted to see me. I'm sorry I was so caught up with my new toy. I kind of blew you off. Come, sit, do you want something to drink?"

He handed Adam a coke, and was ready to listen. A few weeks ago Adam would have left or might have told Vic to go fuck himself, but he was mellowing into a more reasonable human. He told him about his session with Tom and how he came to understand what had happened. Vic listened, tilted back in his chair, hands folded over his chest, fingers interlocked and eyes closed. Adam thought he was either drifting off or communing with the ghost of Sigmund Freud, but when Adam finished, Vic was right there with a big smile.

"That's pretty amazing. You came to this on your own, tapping into your own feelings. That's wonderful, the best and most convincing way to learn. The next step is what do you do with what you know. How do you test it out and use it to help Tom?" Vic went on, putting Adam's experience into a bloodless conceptual model that sucked all the joy out of what he learned on his own. Adam thought what he said was helpful but Vic's patronizing pompous tone was more than he could bear. The difference was that Adam was indeed changing.

He made a quick trip to the ward to tell Tom that he was off for the weekend. Tom reassured him, he was OK and felt safe on the ward. The staff was starting to like Tom and he was feeling at home. He thanked Adam for stopping in and wished him a good weekend. Adam thought Tom was getting better.

He left feeling that he really liked Tom. Maybe the kind of love Dr. G had for him.

■ ■ ■

9

Meeting Lillian at the ER, going for a swim before dinner was beginning to feel a part of Adam, a part he never wanted to change. Even his scars seemed less ugly, he was feeling less ugly inside. He was falling in love, beginning to be able to love himself and forgive himself for what he had done. He thought Goodman was right. There must be a lot of guilt somewhere inside him, but talking about the killings didn't seem to change how he felt about himself. It was being with Lillian that was fueling the change.

At dinner he told her about his work with Tom. "Tom's feelings and thoughts are so magnified that it's like looking at how a mind works under a high powered microscope…it's also helping me understand myself."

" How's it helping you understand yourself?"

"Well it's not just working with Tom, it's also meeting you. I know we just met but I'm having loving feelings for you. It changes the way I feel about myself. Maybe it sounds a little crazy, but if I can love then I must not be so terrible...I'm beginning to realize how unlovable I feel, sort of like an untouchable. It's hard to believe anyone would want to touch me...then you touch me, and your not repulsed." Tears were flowing down Lillian's cheeks. She reached across the table, put her hand on his.

"Adam, we're so much alike. You make me feel lovable too. I haven't felt loveable for a long time."

They spent the rest of dinner mostly smiling at each other, basking in each other's glow, and the night at Adam's place, holding each other with his penis still living a life of its own. Lillian thought they ought to give it a name and they decided on Reb, short for rebellious, since it wouldn't obey the holding only rules.

They slept entwined through the night without the intrusive dreams, and awoke almost on cue, smiling. Adam thought he was dreaming. It was too good to be true. There hadn't been any joy in his life for so long he forgot how it felt. He kept waiting for the shadow of the cloud that followed him around.

They started off at a breakfast place Lillian knew, then she took him on a tour of the neighborhood. He discovered where he could get his laundry done, shop for groceries, get a haircut and have a choice of places to eat. There were several movie theatres he didn't know existed.

"Lillian, you're opening new worlds for me. I didn't realize what's out there once you get off campus."

"Well, you've only been living here for little over a year." She put her arm around his waist. "I couldn't resist that crack. I may know the neighborhood but you're the first man I've been with in a very long time." They walked arms around each other — Lillian stopped and pressed herself against him. "I don't know what's in the future for us but I do know that right now we're good for each other." She gave him one of her pleasure-full smiles. "So, let's buy some furniture."

———

Adam thought Lillian was right, they were good for each other. He would wake up in the morning with energy and enthusiasm that eluded him for years. He could furnish his apartment that had been bare for over a year and he was beginning to get a handle on how terrible he felt about himself. Although his dreams were ever present, he was not as vigilant or as easi-ly startled. He still had the uncontrollable compulsion to wash his hands at about the same time almost every afternoon. It would creep up on him at about three — he would have no peace until he satisfied the inner command to wash.

Over the last few weeks his colleagues commented on how he seemed to be happier with the world. He and Lillian were together full time. Except for their on-call nights they were at Adam's place holding each other. They explored and gave each other pleasure in every conceivable way except Old Reb, wasn't allowed an entrance. It was also obvious that Lillian wasn't ready to have Adam in her apartment.

It was a little over a month since they met, six weeks to be exact, and in a session with Dr. Goodman, he said,

"I don't care whether we have intercourse...I don't care whether I ever get into her apartment. I'd love to but that's her issue to deal with. While it sure as hell impacts me, it isn't because of me. Lillian hasn't worked through her trauma. She isn't at peace with herself, but I'm at peace with our relationship. I love her, love being with her...I know she needs her own time for healing. We're helping each other heal."

A few days after his epiphany, he reminded Lillian that it was his monthly Poker-pension-enhancing night and the game often went past midnight. A warm glow came over her along with a matching smile.

"When you're finished come to my place. Call me, I'll tell the security guard to let you in."

It wasn't Adam's style to interpret the meaning or motives of anyone he had a friendship with, or worked with, and he sure wasn't about to with Lillian. It flattens out the relationship, drains it of life and passion. He kissed Lillian and told her he would call.

Adam didn't really feel like going to the Poker game, but he could use the money. He did enjoy the company, except for big Mike, and he was huge. Mike loved to throw his weight around and played Poker the same way — aggressively, with lack of focus. He would get visibly angry when he lost and he was a loser, at least at Poker. This evening Adam found him particularly irritating. He was talking about consulting at the Veterans Hospital. He kept referring to the VA as the "brick tit" and how these guys just want to suck — get something for nothing. Adam about had it.

"You've ever been in the service or combat, Mike?" He thought the tone of his question would shut him up for the night, but it didn't phase him. *faze*

Mike went on. "No. I had a deferment for med school. Most of these guys never went to college."

Adam had to restrain himself while Mike went on about the Vets he saw at the hospital. He was holding fourth as the cards were being dealt and betting went on. Adam didn't know if Mike was paying attention or not, but he had a possible heart flush. Mike was raising and re-raising. The game was seven card stud and Adam was keeping track of the cards while Mike was blowing off. Adam had a pair of kings in the hole and one up, as well as a jack of clubs, a three of hearts and two of spades. With the last down card Adam drew a jack of spades giving him a full house. Mike

had a four, five and six of hearts showing, the seven
had been played and Adam had the three so he knew
Mike couldn't have a straight flush. There were three
left in the pot and the third folded after Adam raised
Mike. There was at least five hundred in the pot and
Adam knew he had him. When Mike looked at his
hole cards again, Adam thought he might not even
have a flush if he couldn't remember what he had. On
Adam's re-raise, Mike folded.

"So Adam, what did you have?"

"You didn't pay to see 'em, Mike."

have He must of thought that Adam was just giving
him a hard time, or maybe he never took no for an answer. He flashed Adam one of those 'oh come on' smiles
and reached across the table to turn Adam's cards over.
He was shocked when Adam clamped down hard on
his hand. The smile vanished, the silence in the room
was deafening. They stared at each other. Mike looked
like he wanted to kill — Adam hoped he'd try. Finally
Adam said,

"You didn't pay the price to see my cards just like
you didn't pay the price to bad mouth the veterans.
You don't get something for nothing." He released
Mike's hand and waited to see if he wanted to take
it any further. Mike sat and stared. Adam flipped his
cards over. "A full house. Kings over Jacks." Adam
cashed his chips, thanked the host and the rest of guys.

There hadn't been a word uttered from the moment he grabbed Mike's hand to the time he left.

Adam felt good calling Mike on his Poker etiquette and his bad mouthing the Vets. He felt proud he was able to restrain himself from going over the top, although his Poker group may not have thought so. He'd see if he was invited back.

■ ■ ■

It was a little before eleven when he arrived at Lillian's and realized he hadn't called her to let her know he was on his way. He pushed the intercom button.

"I'm Adam Burns to see Dr. Silver." He could see the guard pick up the phone to call Lillian. "Please apologize for me, for not calling her."

"OK, I apologized for you. Bring your bike in and I'll store it."

Jan, the security guard, stored his bike, looked him over, smiled and led him to the elevator.

"This elevator goes to the penthouse. I have to activate the button." She inserted a key in the top unmarked button. "OK. You're all set."

Adam thanked her and asked if he had to get unlocked to come down.

She smiled. "No, but if it doesn't work out with Lillian you know where I work."

He was smiling as the door slid shut and was expressed to the top. It was one of those elevators that take off so you think you left part of yourself behind. There were two doors on the elevator and when one opened he was looking at Lillian dressed in a turquoise blouse, black silky shorts and sandals.

"Welcome to my extravagant digs." She kissed him and handed him a glass of white wine. Adam hadn't said a word. "I hope I haven't thrown you into shock but this is where I hang out."

They clinked glasses and Adam took a sip of a very good wine. "Not in shock, just speechless. Why didn't you give me a heads up?"

"I didn't know how to describe how I live...I was afraid of putting you off. I don't want to lose you."

He wrapped her in his arms and held her close. "That's not going to happen."

Adam could feel the tears on her cheeks as he held her — soothing, reassuring, making it safe.

Lillian gave Adam a tour of her apartment which took up half of the top floor of the building. The other half was used for the family business. They sat, ate, drank and Lillian told him about the investment company her family owned.

"So Adam, I'm not only an educated aggressive woman, but a very rich one to boot. That puts some men off."

"That shouldn't be a concern because you're looking at a man who is loaded." Adam laid all his cash on the table. "I hit it big tonight." He told Lillian about Mike and how the last hand played out. "I don't think he thought I was serious about not showing my hand...I don't think he expects people to push back. It felt good about confronting Mike, but a little badly for causing the others some discomfort. I would love to be that proverbial fly on the wall to see what happened after I left."

"It's a good thing for Mike that you weren't packin."

"It's a good thing for me Mike wasn't packing. If looks could kill I wouldn't be here now."

They were sitting in cushy swivel chairs, facing each other, with their feet up on a hassock, caressing each others toes. Adam took a sip of wine.

"How do you feel having me here?"

She huddled her legs around his. "The invitation just popped out but I knew that I wanted you to come to my place. I want you in my place, Adam, but what I want is maybe something I can't do yet. It may take more time. At least I'm able to let you in the door."

"It wouldn't be true if I said I knew what it felt like to be raped. I can only imagine it...that's horrible enough." He slid over to Lillian and sat astride her, nose to nose. "I hope some day you'll be able to let me inside you, if that meant you were healing, but as far as I'm concerned I've never felt closer to anyone than I do you. I don't have to be inside you to be inside you...don't think I'm not scared...I don't have a clue as to why." He kissed her. She kissed back. The phone rang, she didn't pick-up until she heard her father's voice.

"Hi Dad. Adam is here, I'm putting you on speakerphone so he can hear your wonderful voice."

"Hello Adam, good to meet you but what are you doing in my daughter's apartment?"

"Well Mr. Silver, I don't know what to say except I'm falling in love with your daughter."

Lillian broke in. "We've been together everyday for over a month, tonight is the first time Adam has seen were I live. He now knows in addition to my being beautiful and smart I'm also rich."

"Well I hope that doesn't put him off. Your mother, sister and I are coming to town for the board meeting. We can meet Adam then."

"I get the feeling I'm in for a serious look-over."

He laughed. "You betcha. But it's a two way street. I'll look forward to meeting you, but now you need to take me off speaker phone so I can discuss some business with you, Lilly babe."

When he said goodbye, Adam searched for the bathroom and found it just where he thought it ought to be. He liked the sound of Lillian's father's voice. When he said, "You betcha", he left no doubt what his daughter meant to him. He was smiling when he reemerged and found a smiling Lillian waiting.

"You got a sample of my Dad. He liked the sound of your voice."

"I liked the sound of him too, including the 'you betcha'."

"Are you up for the family inspection?"

"I'd be disappointed if there wasn't one. I'm kind of cocky. I always think everyone will like me."

It was almost one in the morning when they both reached their limit for talk. Adam followed Lillian into her bedroom suite and the luxurious bath and shower. They washed, caressed, loved each other under multi-pulsating faucets of soft warm water and then, exhausted, found their way to the largest bed Adam had ever been in, under silky sheets he could learn to love. They drifted off pressing close, face to face, kissing, soothing each other to sleep.

Any sleep without the bombs and helicopters, was a precious gift and this night was to be very special. Adam didn't know what time it was when old Reb found himself surrounded by Lillian's lips and coaxed to life by the gentle movement of her tongue. He helped her slide over him so he could give her the gift she was giving him. He loved the smell of her and they soared as one into a place of ecstatic joy.

They were back in each others arms, into a blissful sleep, when he heard a whisper. "Adam, are you awake? Adam."

"I think I may be dreaming. I keep hearing this voice in my head." He could feel her smiling.

"Adam, would you do something for me?"

"Anything."

"Would you let me put you inside me and once your inside not move...just be there?"

"Of course. I won't move but I may come. I don't think I can control that."

"That's OK...just don't move...I'm sorry to make this into an experiment...I need to see how it feels. It's crazy isn't it?"

"Not crazy. I think you're trying to desensitize yourself. It feels good I can help. Take charge. Do what you want and can do."

Lillian took hold of him and Adam felt like he was lending her his penis, as a part of a crucial experiment. He felt honored that she could use him in this way and once more realized how they were both part of the cure for each other. He didn't want to think about what might happen once cured or even if that could happen. He was as still as he could be as she sat astride him, slowly putting him inside her, at her will. She had him deep inside when the tears came falling on his chest.

"Thank you Adam. I didn't know if I could ask you to do this. I felt crippled... now I feel fixable." They kissed. "Can you stay in me for a while longer?"

He hugged her close and they spent the rest of the night locked together. Lillian slept. Adam remained in a twilight zone thinking what just happened helped him as much as it helped Lillian.

Waking up was the easy part, getting out of bed was another story. They managed to disengage and get themselves to the shower, which brought them back to the reality of the day ahead.

■ ■ ■

Adam had been meeting with Tom everyday, as well as weekends when he was on call. When Adam would ask Tom whether Lithium was helping him, which he did every time they met, Tom would smile and tell him that he sounds like a nervous mother hovering over her sick child, who she fears will not recover. On this day he smiled, as Adam awaited for the usual rejoinder, and said,

"Adam, I think it is helping. The last few days I've noticed that my mind has slowed down. I don't have thoughts racing through my head; they seem more connected. I can focus better and I'm not rhyming or clanging unconnected sounds. I got a kick out of that, but not being able to control it drove me crazy."

"Sounds like part of you is missing the high."

"Yeah, but I want my mind back. I've been reading the articles you brought me and the more I learn about Manic-Depression, the more I realize my father had it in spades and maybe my brother had a touch also. I hope I don't slip into a depression."

Adam thought it odd he referred to his brother in the past tense. He decided to follow up on it.

"Tom, you said your brother had a touch of it." Adam's tone was questioning and he waited for Tom's reaction. It came loud and clear.

" Fuck you, Adam."

Tom was silent. The tears started as he began to sob.

"He's dead goddamn it. He crashed his fucking plane in the Atlantic ocean. The mother-fucker left me. He's gone."

Adam didn't know what to say. He felt stopped in his tracks. All along he thought that Tom's brother was out to kill him, now he says his brother is dead and he's sobbing uncontrollably. Adam sat with him, restraining himself from handing him a tissue. He needed to cry. He would stop when he was ready. Tom reached over, took a tissue, then handed the box to Adam. That's when Adam first noticed his own tears. He thought this amazing man was still looking after him, even in the midst of his own anguish.

He wanted to ask Tom about his brother, perhaps his name, for starters, but decided not to push it, opting to let Tom set the pace. He had a strong urge to reach out to touch and hold Tom.

"I'm sorry, Tom. I'm so sorry." They sat in silence. Adam at a loss of what to say or do. They sat, bonding with each other, then Tom said,

"I'm OK Adam. I know you need to be someplace. I'll be OK."

"Sometimes I think you can read my mind."

"It comes from having to be on the lookout for any sudden change in the people who are supposed to take care of you. I trust you more than I trust most people, but I'm always tuned in."

When he left Tom he rode his bike to a small park near Dr. Goodman's office. He had a little more than a half hour before his appointment and needed the time to unwind. So he sat and watched the pigeons swarm about an old man who was feeding them. They were all over him, no manners, he was totally focused on making sure each one got their fair share, shooing off the greedy ones, beckoning to the shy stand offs. Adam got back on his bike while still absorbed in how this man was connecting with his extended family. He was standing, shaking his empty bag of crumbs, saying goodbye to each and telling them he would see them tomorrow. Adam waved to him as he rode off but the old man was totally involved with his wards.

Adam noted Dr. G seemed to be in good spirits, then had the thought, "I'm just like Tom. I got to the point, or at least think so, where I can read how he's feeling. If I think he's feeling bad I think it's my fault. I think it's crazy but I really think that way." His thoughts were distracting, he didn't know where to begin. Lillian or Tom? He started with Lillian and told

Dr. G what happened, every detail, while staying glued to his face, waiting for any change, any sign of what he thought. When he finished, Dr. Goodman said,

"You and Lillian, are very good for each other...you're helping each other heal. You're both so loving and generous with one another. It's lovely to hear. Thank you for sharing it with me."

"Really?"

"No, not really. I just said that to make you feel good."

Adam started to laugh and ended up crying.

"What are you feeling?"

Between sobs and heaves he managed to squeeze out, "Relief. That's what I feel, relieved."

"Adam, you watch me like a hawk for any sign that I don't like you. You're waiting for the axe to fall."

"I feel so ugly inside. I can't believe Lillian really loves me. Or you either."

There was a long silence. "So where's the reassurance?"

Dr. G didn't say anything. After awhile he asked, "What are you thinking? Feeling?"

"I was thinking you're withholding." Adam smiled, "Actually I thought you're a withholding prick." He looked at Dr. G.

"I just thought of Mike, and the card game and my telling you that he looked at me as if he wanted to kill me. I didn't tell you I was wishing he'd try."

"What if he tried?"

"If he came at me across the table I had it in mind to grab him by his hair and smash his face into the table." Adam was quiet — waiting for him to say something and when he didn't, he said, "I know that you're going to say there's a difference between thinking and doing." Adam was imitating him and mocking him, ala Tom. *à la* They sat — Adam was boiling inside. "OK Doc. You don't know what I'm capable of doing. What I've done."

"You haven't told me yet." Dr. G waited a moment. "Maybe next time?"

Adam left without the usual goodbye and when he was riding back to the hospital he vowed he would never go back. There was nothing to tell. It was all in the past, buried, he wasn't going to dig any of it up. He grazed a bush on the side of the bike path and almost lost control of the bike. He thought he needed to put all this shit out of his head and concentrate *on* staying on the path. Usually, by the time he reached the hospital his mind would be thoroughly cleansed, but not today. He kept thinking of how the session ended. "What I've done", kept rattling around inside his head. He noticed a rip in his pants leg and a small abrasion. He thought of going to the ER to have Lillian make it all better. The image of a little boy crying to his mom brought him back to the real world.

A feeling of profound fatigue set in. Adam had to drag himself to the ward, forcing himself to stay focused for a staff meeting. He listened, made some suggestions, asked some questions and wrote some orders for meds and procedures. He was about to leave when Sarah Johnston, the charge nurse, asked to meet with him. Sarah, a women in her mid-fifties, was a natural for the job and she could read Adam's mood like she was inside his head.

"Adam, you're barely with us today. Did you have another of those intense sessions with Tom?"

Adam was taken by surprise when he started to tear up. "Not with Tom. It's about me. I'm getting in touch with some of my past. I've done a pretty good job of forgetting and it's starting to come back." He didn't know if he was imagining that Sarah asked what it was that was coming back or that he was just ready to tell someone else. "It's just some leftovers from my time in the service."

"Those leftovers can be pretty powerful. I know... I was a surgical nurse in a MASH unit in Korea."

He was speechless. "Sarah, you may have taken care of me."

"You're smiling but I very well could have."

"Maybe you've got a formula for putting all this shit in the past, for good. It keeps popping up."

"I haven't found the formula yet but it gets less powerful... loses some of its impact, but it took a while."

"That's what my shrink keeps telling me."

"That's what Dr. Goodman told me also. He's right, the scars do get less sensitive." She saw his look of surprise. "I see him every once in awhile now... one day I saw you leaving his office. He's known for his understanding of trauma, so it wasn't hard to put it all together. I really can't read your mind."

"Wow, that's a relief."

"Adam, I've joined a group of health professionals who've been exposed to various kinds of trauma, and I'm finding it very helpful. I'm not sure how but I think we're helping each other. If you're interested I'll ask the group if they want a new member."

"Thanks Sarah...not just yet...maybe sometime down the road." He was getting his energy back. "It was helpful talking with you but I'm not ready for a group of people I don't know." He squeezed her hand. "Thanks."

He left the psych pavilion and found a shady spot under one of the large red maples that dotted the campus. He thought he should take a leave of absence until he straightens his head out. Better yet, commit himself to the lock ward and share a room with Tom.

From where he was sitting he had a good view of the psych building as well as the new hospital. All the old buildings had been demolished and every service moved to the new hospital, except psychiatry. He thought, "This old building with its added on air conditioners that stick out like old warts, is like saying Psychiatry is the asshole of medicine. Nobody wants to have anything to do with crazy people or anyone connected with them. The same with the Corps. I get a medical retirement for my leg and half a lung but not for what's wrong with my head. No Marine ever has mental problems. Ya gotta be crazy to think that."

———

He wasn't particularly hungry but thought if Lillian got off for lunch he might see her in the cafeteria. When he got closer to the hospital he could see a lot of flashing lights pulling into the ER and knew Lillian wasn't going to make lunch. It was Adam's on-call night. Lillian was going to meet him for dinner and spend the night. He'd have to wait until then, but he couldn't resist a peek. It's the same impulse that brings traffic to a halt so everyone can get a look at an accident scene. One look told Adam, this was a mother of an accident. They were wheeling people in like they just opened the doors for a summer sale. Lillian was moving from gurney to gurney deciding who needed immediate attention. He felt possessive, really proud of his Lillian, who was in charge. Then the cloud descended and he was thinking she's a real doc and real doc's get to move into the new hospital. He couldn't believe what he was thinking. He felt like a two year old screaming for the ice cream cone the other kids had. He felt like he was turning beet red and needed to get the hell out of there.

His first impulse was to have a cigarette and a drink to calm down. Just this once to collect himself. The shame of having to tell Dr. G and Lillian was worse than sitting with what he was feeling. He headed for the cafeteria. Maybe some coffee or something will help or maybe just being around people. He wasn't in a very charitable mood as he stood in line looking at the fat asses who couldn't control their appetites, completely ignoring that a few minutes ago he was going out to smoke himself to death and get bombed out of his mind. He grabbed a sandwich, and a coke and found a table out of the way of everyone. One by one his residency group found their way to his hidden table which turned out to be a gift in disguise. He could lose himself in conversation and get outside of his own bellybutton, at least for the moment. Today was Bob Hansen's twenty-seventh birthday and Brenda was handing out ice cream bars for the occasion. There was the teasing about his getting older, which led to a round of everyone telling their age. Brenda was the youngest by a few months, Eric and Steve were twenty-seven, Vic was thirty and Adam became the focus of the old man jokes at thirty-four. At that moment he felt like a toddler who had just been toilet trained, and hoped it didn't show. He was able to lose himself in the mindless conversation which turned out to be fun and in a strange way, soothing. It stifled his aloneness.

■ ■ ■

Lillian had been on the move for three hours without a break. She was putting a chest tube in a girl who looked to be about twelve. She was a passenger in a car that was sandwiched in the middle of a pile up. At last count twenty cars and a tractor-trailer were involved. She kept asking if her mother was OK. Lillian reassured her, that her mom was being taken care of, even though she had no idea where her mother was.

"Cheryl, as soon as I get you taken care of I'll check on your mom." Cheryl had a large bump on her forehead and Lillian was worried about a closed head injury. She left orders for a skull film and for vital signs to be checked every fifteen minutes along with keeping tabs on her pupils. "We're going to clean up those cuts on your face and nose and have a plastic surgeon take a look, so you can leave looking beautiful. I'm going to find your mom, and tell her you're OK," and to the nurse, "Let me know when Cheryl's blood work comes back. If it's not back in the next fifteen minutes call the lab."

Lillian made a quick check of all the patients in the hall — seeing if any were in acute distress or pain — reassuring them they hadn't been forgotten. She grabbed the charge nurse, Marge Rouse, "Marge can you take a sec?" Marge slowed to a walk. "What do you think about putting one of our techs in charge of the hall to keep check on vital signs until we get everyone treated…get someone out in the waiting room talking to the people waiting…maybe get some liquids out there…juice…let them know about wait times."

Marge gave her a look, like she's running her ass off what do you want from me, "OK Lillian, but we're not taking in laundry."

Lillian went out to the waiting room where about fifty people were milling around. "Hey, listen up good people. I'm Dr. Silver…I apologize for the wait time. We're working with the most serious injuries first. We're going to get you something to drink and if anyone is in unbearable pain or feels like they're in trouble let us know. In the meantime start talking with each other. That helps during times like this."

She went back to check the treatment rooms and found Cheryl's mom who was getting her left arm casted. She also had a contusion to the left side of her head where she must have hit the window on the driver's side. "Hi Mrs. Brown. I'm Dr. Silver. I just left Cheryl, she's fine." Lillian saw the relief on her face. "I want to tell you what we did to take care of Cheryl."

Lillian described Cheryl's injuries, the need for a chest tube to drain her chest cavity and re-inflate her lung. "We'd like to keep her overnight to make sure she's OK…from the looks of that contusion on your head you ought to join her. We'll get you together as soon as the cast is set."

It was past three before the ER was back to normal. Lillian wanted to meet with the staff while everything was still fresh in their minds. She ordered drinks, a sandwich tray from the cafeteria and got everyone together in the conference room. She waited until everyone was settled with food and drink.

"OK. I'm really proud of all of you. We worked like a great team. I found out that it was more like sixty cars involved in the pile up…we got the overflow from City Hospital. This is the most trauma injuries we've had since I've been here…we all did well. While it's still fresh I'd like to hear what your reactions are. What you think we did right and what we can do better."

It was slow to get started but to Lillian's surprise the feelings started pouring out. How it felt to be under the gun, especially dealing with the bleeders, head injuries and badly broken bones. Finally they seemed to wind down and then Marge Rouse piped up with, "I was kind of pissed when you grabbed me in the hall. I'm running my ass off and you're telling me to get a monitor in the hall and drinks in the waiting room."

There was a silent moment, waiting for Lillian to respond.

"So, Marge, why don't you tell me how you really feel."

"Well I was going to. I was pissed but when I saw the calming effect it had on everyone I thought it was a pretty good idea and was glad I thought of it." The laughter helped everyone decompress and triggered a flood of suggestions making the ER more user friendly. Lillian wanted to give Marge a great big hug, so when everyone cleared out, she did.

———

Lillian was in the staff lounge getting dressed, when Leslie Dillon came in and handed her an envelope.

"That's a letter of resignation. I can stay until the end of the month if you want me to."

Lillian was surprised as well as relieved. "It would be helpful if you stayed until then. Leslie, I want you to know, I've always thought you are a first rate physician, but I have a problem about your putting your personal beliefs ahead of established protocols and procedures."

"I know Lillian. I knew it was a matter of time when we would clash again. I accepted an ER position at Good Samaritan where I would be more in synch with hospital policy."

"Good for you. I wish you well."

They shook hands and Lillian got a smile and a God bless.

■ ■ ■

Adam sauntered into the ER looking for Lillian and found there was a patient waiting for him. Lillian was going to catch up on some paper work, then they would have dinner in the hospital cafeteria.

The patient, Stanley Rubin, was a man in his early thirties who looked as if he was in a fog and not very verbal. His wife, Cindy, said for the last few weeks he has not been himself. He has no energy to do the things he usually took pleasure in, such as a daily run in the park that they did together, or playing with their new Lab puppy. She said, "He's just not here. He sits as he is right now…he doesn't seem to connect." She went on to describe his forgetting what he was about to say and has difficulty coming up with the names of common everyday things. He's become worse in the last few days and hasn't been able to work. They're both accountants who work together out of an office in their home. The quality of his work has deteriorated to the point where she had to take over. She also has had to help him with his personal hygiene.

Adam started to evaluate the man's cognitive functions and could see his wife trying to restrain herself from jumping in to help him with questions he couldn't answer. He knew his name but guessed at the date, day of the week and was off on both. He had a pronounced impairment of immediate recall, couldn't repeat anything he was asked to remember and was at a loss ~~of how to do~~ simple arithmetic. His memory for past events was also impaired and as he tried to converse it was obvious he had an expressive aphasia. When asked to identify familiar objects, such as a pen, pencil, notepad he looked like he knew what they were but just couldn't come up with the name. With every difficulty he was so frustrated with himself he would slap his forehead as if he could shake the word loose. Adam thought this man had something organic causing his problems. He did a physical exam and the only abnormal finding was on examining his eyes. He had papilledema of both optic discs. The margins of the optic nerves were completely blurred. A sign of increased intracranial pressure.

Adam thought, "Oh shit, this poor guy probably has a brain tumor...how the hell am I going to tell him and his wife." Adam started to have split second flashbacks of writing letters to families of men he lost. Cindy Rubin picked up on Adam's discomfort.

"You don't have good news for us, do you?"

Adam regained the moment. "Mrs. Ruben, I think your husband has something causing increased pressure in his head which is effecting his abilities to function. *affecting* All the things you've told me about." Adam realized he was talking to her as if her husband wasn't in the room so he took Mr. Rubin's hand and asked him if he understood what he had just told his wife. He nodded. He looked blank and she looked terrified. Adam moved his chair closer where he could look at and talk to both. He asked if they had a private doctor he could call. They didn't have one.

"I would recommend Mr. Ruben come into the hospital so we can run some tests, get some x-rays, to see what's causing this increased pressure."

After a silent exchange of looks, Mrs. Ruben summoned her voice. "OK. Do you have any idea what's wrong?"

"The most likely thing is a tumor that's pressing on the brain. We need to get a neurosurgical consult and get things going." Adam was looking at two people in shock. "Maybe I shouldn't have told you what I think without more tests…I wanted to be upfront with you. This is serious but not a death sentence. Tumors are often operable and can be removed. So let's see what the neurosurgeon says."

While they waited for the neurosurgeon, Adam brought them a pitcher of water, and let them talk. It didn't take much for them to connect and pretty soon they were on a first name basis. Stan and Cindy Ruben have been married for three years and built a substantial accounting practice. They've been considering having a family but they're not quite ready. Cindy did the talking but it was clear that Stan understood what she was saying and would nod his head to signal his agreement. Adam was getting a good idea of how they related to each other and what their lives were like before Stan's symptoms made their appearance and turned everything upside down. Cindy was telling Adam about a bike trip they took and looking back on it realized that Stan wasn't at his best, when the door swung open and the neurosurgeon made his appearance. At least Adam assumed he was the neurosurgeon. He was in scrubs with no ID showing and he didn't introduce himself. As he reached for Stan's chart he reminded Adam of Mike reaching across the table to turn his cards over. Adam snatched the chart before he could get to it.

"You need to identify yourself before you get to see this man's medical records."

He had the same shocked look as Mike did, but he did back off and spit out his name.

"I'm Dr. Rademyer, senior neurosurgical resident." He spoke in clipped tones which matched his wired look. He stood tilted back like he needed to keep his distance and gave the appearance that he was looking down his nose. Adam was not getting good vibes and felt protective of the Rubens.

"I'm Dr. Burns, junior psychiatric resident…this is Mr. and Mrs. Ruben." He handed the chart to him, and waited. Dr. Rademyer turned toward Stan Ruben, never making direct eye contact, and started asking questions with his nose buried in the chart. His manner was gruff and devoid of compassion or respect. Adam couldn't believe what he was seeing.

"Dr. Rademyer, please step out in the hall. We need to talk." He opened the door and Rademyer got the message that he wasn't asking. Adam had a hard edge to his voice.

"Let me spell this out for you. These people are in shock facing news that's turning their life upside down. You either go in there and treat them with respect and whatever compassion you can muster or get your ass out of here…I can get someone else to consult with." Adam watched and waited and then it dawned on him. "You don't know what the hell I'm talking about…do you?" Rademyer looked at Adam as if he had descended from outer space. "I'm going to talk with the Rubens and see how they want to go. We'll call if we need you."

Rademyer was left standing in the hall looking like a child who had been sent to the principal and didn't know what the offence was.

need transition to get L in picture

Adam told the Rubens what he had done and told them he would like to find them a surgeon who could relate to them and follow Stan through his recovery. Lillian recommended a neurosurgeon who agreed to see Stan, and he would meet them in the ER of the hospital where he worked. When they left Cindy squeezed Adam's hand and thanked him. He felt like he was on a high, a feeling that lasted until he spied Rademyer, with a backup, at the front desk talking with Lillian.

Lillian greeted Adam with, "Dr. Burns, this is Dr. Strickland, Chief Resident of Neurosurgery. You already met Dr. Rademyer. They want to talk to you."

Strickland, a tall intense looking guy, went into a rant about how Adam *had* treated his resident. He was getting off on how this is a teaching hospital and how Dr. Rademyer was deprived of a good case by referring the patient out of the system. He said the Department of Neurosurgery had an international reputation for excellence and that the patient would have had the best of care. Adam waited until he ran out of gas.

"Well, that's all very interesting but you haven't asked me why I asked Dr. Rademyer to leave and referred the patient to someone else." Adam tried to paint the picture of someone in shock having heard life changing news, in the language that might penetrate his surgical vest. He compared Rademyer's behavior toward someone who has just heard they may have a brain tumor, to someone bursting into their operating room unannounced, inspecting an open wound with un-scrubbed hands. He could see that he wasn't getting through to him so he summed it all up with, "In any case, this is not medicine practiced at its best."

They looked at Adam with disbelief, then at each other. They left without another word. Adam thought he'd better document all of what happened and make a copy to give Vic.

On the way to the cafeteria Lillian gave him a hug. "We're becoming the champions of all the victims of trauma, aren't we?" She gave him another hug. "Some of my staff think I'm over the top providing drinks for people waiting in the ER. I can't wait to see what they're going to say when I start passing out cookies."

"Ah, I love it. I love being a crusader. We'll both get canned or locked-up but as long as we're locked-up together it's OK."

They had a great time eating mediocre food, on a table covered with paper napkins, lighting imaginary candles and toasting their cause with glasses of ice tea. Lillian spent the night with Adam in the on-call room where they fell a sleep curled together as close as they could be.

It was four in the morning when Adam bolted upright, covered with sweat, his heart going a mile a minute and his repeating over an over, "What have I done…what have I done?"

He was inspecting his hands when Lillian whispered, "Adam, I think you had one of those dreams. It's OK. You're OK."

He sat on the edge of the bed while Lillian wiped his face with a cool wash cloth. "I remember parts of the dream...I had done something and I was looking at my hands...they were dripping with blood...I was screaming what have I done. I think that's what I was saying when I woke up." Lillian took his hands and kissed them. It took all the reserve he could muster not to pull away. He didn't want to contaminate her.

"Lillian, there's blood on my hands." She put her finger to his lips. "I have to tell you...you have to know this about me. I've managed to hide it from myself for too long." She was silent but held his hands, lovingly and firmly. "It's pretty amazing how I've been able to file this away as if it never happened." She waited. "It was the middle of winter and there was fresh snow on the ground. I thought it was a good time to reconnoiter. We could move quietly in the snow...I took five men." He paused to catch his breath. He was hyperventilating. "We nearly stumbled into a group of North Koreans. They were camped in a rock enclave and they had eleven Marines with their hands bound behind them. They were sitting back to back in the snow. We counted twelve of them huddled around a fire with two sentries posted at the natural entry ways. We backed off to decide what to do." Lillian handed him a glass of water. He took a sip. He felt an unreal stillness as if he were back in Korea. "We surrounded their camp. I was going to take out one of the sentries and my sergeant would get the other. We'd yell for the Marines to hit the deck and come in and take out the North Koreans before they could get to their weapons. That's exactly what we did." He took another sip of water. "We freed the prisoners...one was a Navy Corpsman. He thought I was wounded. I was covered with the blood of the sentry I took down. I had my hand over his mouth and slit his throat. He was pumping out blood as I held him and then slowly lowered him to the ground. We didn't take prisoners. Any wounded still alive we finished off, so they couldn't call for help and block our escape." Adam was talking fast, as if he stopped he wouldn't be able to utter another word. He looked at Lillian. She was still holding his hands, still with him. He had to tell her more, like it wasn't horrific or revolting enough. "I was carrying this kid...he couldn't have been more than eighteen or nineteen. He was on my back...holding on...moaning in my right ear...in a lot of pain...I kept telling him we were almost home like you would tell a little boy...all of a sudden his moans changed to a hum...he was humming the Marine hymn. We got back to base camp and celebrated. The freed Marines were all over us. We drank beer until it was coming out of our ears...even the kid I carried out was evacuated with a beer can in one hand. We burned my blood soaked fatigues and danced around the fire. We were heroes...we all got medals. I was promoted and a few months later awarded the Silver Star." He stopped talking. The tears took over. Silent tears. Mournful tears. Remorseful tears. Lillian was still holding his hands, kissed the tears and held him close. He whispered to her. "Until tonight I kept the look of the Korean kid pumping blood all over me in a concrete vault...I've been living under a cloud...feeling so ugly inside no one would ever be able to love me."

She held him close, face to face, and said, "I love you Adam Burns."

"Thank you Lillian Silver. I love you too."

■■■

Lillian and Adam lingered over breakfast. They were not eager to part. Each day they were discovering each other anew, it was cementing an emerging bond turning fragments of the past into a more solid foundation for the future. He left her with the memory of the night intact with a strange feeling of weightlessness. The horrors that plagued him finally brought to light, in the present, freed a part of him which had been in bondage. It was like Tom getting his mind back.

At rounds, he was pleased at how his mind was working. He could tell the story of his encounter with the neurosurgeons and referring the Rubens out of the University system, without his usual punch reminiscent of a round in a boxing match. Vic was supportive and pleased Adam had it all documented.

On his way to see Tom, he was wondering how much of his mind Tom could actually read, and wasn't surprised when he was greeted with, "Adam, you look less burdened today."

Adam smiled. "Yeah, I'm feeling pretty good. How about you?"

"I'm getting my mind back. I think the Lithium is working and helping me think more clearly…my head isn't all cluttered up…but I've also been thinking about our relationship. I haven't figured it out yet, but knowing you has brought me a peace of mind that I haven't had for a long time. I think it has to do with who you are and how it ties in with losing my brother. Does that sound crazy?" Before Adam could say anything he said, "No, it's not crazy. Just complicated…….I think I'm ready to tell you about my brother and family."

For the next hour, Tom, told Adam about his family, pausing only to wipe his eyes or to take a drink. He was six years old, killing and blowing up toy soldiers, when he heard two explosions. The first was his father blowing his mother away, with a 12 gauge shotgun and the second was his father blowing his brains all over the room. He ran towards the sounds and was gathered up by his sister just as he entered the room where his parents lay, father on top of mother. He saw enough to make an indelible mark, and haunt him with terrifying dreams for years. He never touched his soldiers again. His sister, Elizabeth, was twenty-one at the time, and took over both the role of mother as well as head of family. Mark, Tom's sixteen year old brother, came home from prep school, and he and Elizabeth became mother and father to Tom.

"I love Elizabeth and I need to call her. She's probably worried to death over me. I don't want her yanking me out of here. I'm not ready to leave yet." He took a sip of water. "I love Elizabeth with all my heart and I was in love with Mark." He waited to see what Adam's reaction would be. Adam smiled and waited. "I adored him...had erotic, romantic dreams about him. I told him I loved him and wanted to make love to him. Anything he wanted from me, I would have gladly given." He started to cry. Adam teared up. He wiped his eyes and as usual handed the box of tissues to Adam. They both smiled. "He wouldn't allow it. He loved me. He said he would never do anything to hurt me. He and Elizabeth knew I was homosexual. They loved me and thought that it was normal for me. I couldn't ask for better parents. They were in a class by themselves. I was glad mother and father were dead. It was horrible when they were alive, drinking and fighting. I was the luckiest queer alive."

He stopped talking and looked at Adam. "Don't you have to go?"

Adam looked at his watch and this incredible man was right on. It was time for him to leave and start out to see Dr. G. "You're an incredible human, Tom. You hand me tissues to wipe my tears, now you're keeping track of time for me. Thank you."

"You're welcome." As he was about to leave he said, "Adam, I could do lots of things for you. I love you." He smiled and laughed. "Don't worry I'm not going to jump you."

Adam left smiling, thinking he really is an incredible person. Tom's loving him didn't make him anxious. He thought Tom must be picking something up he couldn't see in himself. He had never met anyone who was that tuned in.

He thought about Tom all the way to Dr. Goodman's office, completely forgetting about his dream until he parked his bike, then it all came flooding back.

Dr. G was right on time as usual. He was smiling and Adam was trying to read his mood. That made him think of Tom tuning into him. So that's how he started the hour, talking about the similarities between Tom and himself. Then the blood seeped back in.

"Last time when I left I thought I would never come back. I didn't know why exactly…I was angry at you and didn't know why." It was an effort to talk. "Usually by the time I ride back to the hospital I manage to forget the session, or at least most of it. Last time it didn't happen. I couldn't let go of what I said at the end." Adam fell silent.

"What you said was…you didn't know what you were capable of…what you had done."

"I was on-call last night. Lillian slept with me in the on-call room. I had this dream. I was screaming, what have I done, over and over. I was dripping with blood. My hands were covered with blood." He was staring at his hands, quiet, Dr. Goodman handed him a glass of water. He was in a sweat, his heart was pounding just like last night. "I woke up staring at my hands. Lillian was holding me, wiping my face with a cold washcloth. She told me what I was shouting. Everything came back. It's not that I didn't remember, but it all was in cold storage. Sliced up and stored away." It was hard to keep talking. He didn't want to tell it all over again. They sat in silence for a time, when Dr. G reached over and touched his hand.

"Adam, I know it's hard to talk but you need to tell me what you felt, what your memories are. It will help you to work it over, and this may not be the last of it."

Adam told him what he told Lillian. Every detail. He felt outside of himself, as if he was telling a story about someone else, but every once in awhile the feelings would break through and he knew he was talking about himself, about what he had done. He was exhausted and must of looked it.   have

"Adam, we have to stop now. I want to be sure you're OK."

Adam nodded. Dr. G walked him to the front door and watched while he unlocked his bike.

"Be careful riding back. I want to see you tomorrow in one piece."

Adam tried to stay focused on riding, taking extra care avoiding any cracks in the pavement. At the same time he was feeling the weightlessness he felt with Lillian. It was like someone had lifted a heavy weight off his shoulders. He began to realize how crippled he had been and was sampling the joy of feeling better. He thought of Lillian, how wonderful it was he had her in his life. It was time for the pendulum to swing more towards her, to what she needed from him. He floated through the rest of the day, going to meetings, seeing patients on his ward, attending classes with one eye on the clock, as time seemed to drag out forever, keeping him from his love.

Finally, a little after three, he rode his bike over to the ER. Lillian was still briefing her replacement, the ER was in quiet mode with just a handful of patients waiting. He noticed that drinks and cookies were readily available. One corner of the waiting area was set up to keep kids occupied and to screen them from the main corridors, so the blood and guts of trauma victims weren't forced down their throats. Lillian had the idea of dividing the ER into a user friendly walk-in clinic section, separate from the area for acute emergencies. He thought this was on the cutting edge and could change how ERs are managed and set-up. He was running through an outline of an article they could write about a more supportive, efficient way to approach the trauma of illness, when he felt Lillian's hand caressing his neck.

"You were lost in thought."

He turned and kissed her. "I was thinking about the changes you're making in the ER. You ought to write it up and publish your ideas." They started toward the door. "I was really thinking that we ought to write it up."

"I like that better."

They set out for the Athletic Center walking his bike between them making a connection through the handle bars. Lillian's routine of winding down was becoming Adam's as well. They swam. He did twenty laps, then watched Lillian. They showered and both thought there should be coed showers. Lillian sat on the bar of his bike and they rode to her apartment, both agreeing to forgo jokes about the bar.

After a light dinner they went out to the terrace, sipping wine, looking at and thanking the stars they found each other. Adam told her he felt he was too centered on himself and has been neglectful of her.

"Oh Adam, I don't think you realize what you've done for me. I didn't know myself, how unlovable I felt...how I was isolating myself. When I first met you, I don't know what in the world made me say that gorgeous Leslie Dillon was a tight ass and I was more your type." She was laughing so hard, it was contagious. "I just knew we'd be good for each other." She took his face in her hands and softly kissed him, first on the small scar above his right eye, then his nose that was too perfectly reconstructed, then the scar on his chin and then his lips. "It feels loving and tender to have you in me and I'm almost ready to add the motion. How about that for progress?" She laughed again. "You know, I talked about what happened to me over and over for almost five years in therapy...I thought I had come to some kind of peace with it all. And I did, but I couldn't allow myself to have any intimacy with anyone...I had opportunities. Some nice men, but it just didn't click. The same with a few women I was close to. One in particular I thought I was in love with but I couldn't let her touch me the way she wanted to. She left me and said that I was too damaged. I found that I wasn't sexually attracted to women, but I thought they would be better nurturers than men." She refilled her wine glass and took a sip. "There was something about you. Maybe you're right that people who are traumatized are attracted to others who've been. I don't know."

"It feels that way but I don't know either." They were standing close. Looking at the skyline and lights of the city. "You haven't told me what happened to you. Is that because you can't or don't want to talk about it."

"I thought I had but I guess it was an outline without the details. Do you need to know the details?"

"Need? — No — I don't need to know. I want to know you but I don't want to own you...I sure as hell don't see you as damaged goods. Your woman friend didn't know when she had the real thing."

Lillian got another bottle of wine and brought out a platter of cheese and crackers. She sat on the sofa and beckoned him to her. "I think I need to tell you what happened." She sipped her wine. "No, I don't need to, but I want to tell you. I do want you to know me." She passed the cheese platter to him. "Have some wine and cheese. This is a long story. I don't know where to start."

"Start when you were very young. The first memories you have." Lillian looked surprised.

"OK Dr. Burns."

"I'm not playing psychiatrist with you. I'd never do that. Your life didn't start and thankfully didn't end with a rape. I've gotten the feeling that you were a pretty happy kid. Am I right?"

"You know, when I look back on my early times I see a kid who's smiling, running, swimming and into a lot of activities. Busy. I don't remember any big fights with my mom or dad, or even with my sister. I probably had a few knockdowns, but I don't remember any in particular. I'll have to ask them. I just heard they'll be here next weekend and they all want to meet you."

"Oh shit. I'd better get a haircut, maybe some new clothes and maybe sometime before they come, you'll tell me their names."

"I will, I will. I hope you'll like them. I love them. If it weren't for them I don't know if I would've made it." He could see her eyes mist up — his were following suit.

"My life was going great. I would say a nine and-a-half, out of ten. I was doing well in school...had some good friends and found something I was exceptionally good at and loved. I was totally involved in swimming...I was among the top high school swimmers in the state. It was after an all State meet that it happened." Lillian's voice changed. She had slipped out of the role of commentator and was sliding back into the horror of the past, as it came to life again in the present. Adam held her, telling her it was enough. She didn't have to be raped all over again.

"I thought I had put this all to rest. I guess it's always there, never completely goes away. I want to tell you...I want you to know what happened...I want you to know what you have done for me." She sat up, looking at him head on. "Four teens grabbed me as I was leaving the school, threw me in the trunk of their car. I was screaming my head off but no one heard me. They didn't drive far. When the trunk opened we were in an alley. They raped me, sodomized me, punched me in the face when I screamed, and left me lying in my own waste hardly able to move." She paused for a breath and some wine. "Their faces were burned in my mind and I remember saying something like, I'll get you. They laughed, said it was four to one, like my word against the four of them. When I pulled myself together I felt something underneath me. It was a wallet. One of them lost his wallet. It must have fallen out of his pocket when he dropped his pants. I remember thinking that I got you, you bastards. I had a vice-like grip on the wallet, it gave me the strength to get out to the street and start yelling for help. A woman stuck her head out the window yelling, she had called the police. A cab stopped. The cab driver looked after me until the police came. An ambulance took me to the hospital. All the while I had this death-like grip on the wallet...no one tried to take it from me. Two women detectives came into the ER, part of a Rape Team. They took pictures, asked me to give them an account of what happened and to describe the guys. Then one asked if I knew any of them. I remember saying just one and handed her the wallet. She took one look and said, 'Lillian, you got em. They won't get away with what they did to you'. Hearing that felt good. I didn't feel so powerless and the same night the police had all four of them. They were waiting outside the house of the kid who lost his wallet. When he showed up they got him and two others. It didn't take them long to get the fourth." She stopped talking, leaned into Adam. "I'm trying to remember. I think it was the coach who found my duffle. When I wasn't with my family, they called the police, then the whole team and all the families fanned out around the school searching for me. My mom and dad and sister were frantic. The whole group descended on the ER and were outside waiting and cheering when they rolled me in. It felt like I had just won a race and set a record. It felt good that they all cared about me."

Lillian was quiet, Adam thought she probably ran out of gas and had enough for now when she said, "I don't know what was worse the actual rape or the days and months after. I got my rear repaired, my front examined, my nose fixed and my family never left my side. I could feel the rage building everyday. I don't know who had more of it, me or my father. I wanted to kill these kids and he would've been glad to help."

Lillian went back to school a month after the rape, but she stopped swimming. A good deal of time was spent preparing for a trial which became the focus of her life for the next six months. She barely slept. She daydreamed, seeing the faces of the rapists when they were sentenced for long terms in prison. She told Adam of her fantasies of them being raped everyday and being helpless to do anything about it. She read stories written about prison rape and was so obsessed with the thought, she couldn't concentrate on anything else.

"I wasn't eating or sleeping…I was going through the day like a robot with my mind on getting even with these guys. I started therapy with a wonderful woman. She was a holocaust survivor…we clicked right off. Sylvia Brodsky, have you heard of her?"

"Sure. She's a well known psychoanalyst, who's written a lot on trauma."

"I walked into her office and saw this wonderful smile on this lovely looking woman I towered over…I just let go and cried. She held me until I was able to talk…she sat next to me on her couch, while I told her all I can think of was killing these kids. At that first session I saw the numbers tattooed on her arm and over the next five years learned a little of what she had been through in her early teens but most of all it was focused on me. So for the next five years I saw her once a week or five times a week. She left it up to me, most of the time, but she let me know what she thought. I still keep in touch with her."

"Have you told her about us?"

"I haven't spoken with her in a while, but I know she'll be happy for me."

"What happened at the trial.?"

"It never went to trial. All these kids were seventeen, they would be tried as adults. Their lawyers got them to take an offer of ten years, otherwise they would go to trial and probably get twenty. One of them got five years of probation. He hadn't participated in the rape and agreed to testify against the others. The DA said if this wasn't OK with me he would take them to trial. My mom and dad were at the sentencing with me. Three apologized and one was put on probation. He wrote me a long letter of apology. He was ashamed and guilty that he hadn't found someway of stopping them. I think he was sincere. I don't know about the others. They all got out on parole after four years. It was long enough so they got a good feel of what it was like to be powerless." She topped their glasses. "During this time I found Karate, and a Sensei I liked and respected. He's an elderly man from Okinawa who must be in his eighties by now. Between Mr. Tanaka and Dr. Brodsky I began to feel safe and whole again. I was healing, still am and my finding you was…what…luck…intuition…fate?" She kissed him. "Love really does heal."

"I'll drink to that." They finished the wine, showered and went to bed, both exhausted.

■ ■ ■

A dam was working over what Lillian had told him. She seemed more at peace with herself than he was. He could understand her rage at these kids who violated her, but he couldn't get a handle on what was simmering inside of himself. He hadn't been violated. He was the violator and that didn't sit well with him. He was brought off centerfold when he heard Lillian talking on the phone. He listened as she had the other suite stocked with food and prepared for her family. She had a great way of asking people to do things that would be hard to imitate. It's like being asked but told in a way that makes you feel part of the decision. He thought maybe the Corps could learn something about motivating people from her.

On the way to the cafeteria Adam asked if it was OK for her family to know they sleep together, and whether she wanted more space when they were here.

"Adam, I would like you to stay with me but we won't tell them we sleep together and we most certainly don't inhale." She gave him a hug and over breakfast

described
described) sound as if they are actually there

introduced him to Benjamin, Esther and Emily and promised to tell him more about them over dinner.

At morning rounds he found out that the head of neurosurgery had sent a letter to Dr. Martin, complaining about a certain junior resident of psychiatry. Vic sent a copy of Adam's note and was getting the chart for Dr. Martin. Adam was more concerned with being a violator than he was with the complaints of the head of neurosurgery. He also wanted rounds to be over so he could check on what Tom was finding out about Tom. He thought that this man was doing an incredible amount of work on his own.

Tom greeted him at the door. "Good morning Dr. Burns, and before you ask, I'm better than I was yesterday and I don't think it's all the Lithium." When they were alone Tom told Adam he thought the Lithium was working and felt his thinking was as clear as it ever was, but what made the difference in how he felt was their relationship. "It has been two years since I lost Mark. During my craziness I told you he crashed his plane in the Atlantic Ocean. I didn't tell you I was suppose to go with him but I came down with the flu and pneumonia. When he died a part of me died. I came apart at the seams. That's when I went crazy. Mark left a wife and two children. I couldn't face them. I thought I had let them down. If I had been with Mark I would have saved him." He stopped and looked at Adam, as if he were taking a read of what was going through Adam's mind. "You're thinking that's crazy. Oh, I think I know what you're thinking. I know I don't. It's really what I'm thinking." He smiled and Adam waited for the maniacal laughter. It didn't happen. Tom was in command of his thinking and could regulate himself. The force that propelled his thoughts and speech was gone. "Adam, I was totally out of my mind. I heard a voice telling me to retrieve Mark's body from the ocean and then he would come back to life. I was convinced I could do that. I heard a chorus of voices telling me my family was going to kill me...then I would become paralyzed, couldn't move a muscle. I heard the doctors diagnose me as a catatonic schizophrenic one day, a schizo-affective the next and no one tried to talk to me or ask me what I was feeling, or treat me as if I was human, until that night in the emergency room. You were the real deal, Adam. No bullshit, no patronizing and despite the awful smell, you stuck with me. I thought maybe I found someone I can trust because I sure as hell couldn't trust myself."

"Do you think that's why you became paralyzed, because you couldn't trust yourself?"

"Yes. It wasn't my family that wanted to kill me, it was me. I was suicidal. I don't think they got that I was protecting myself from myself. People who are crazy do crazy things." Tom looked at the clock knowing Adam had to leave soon. Adam was sure Tom surmised that he had to see his shrink. "I'm starting to make some sense out of all the craziness. I do want to call Elizabeth. I'm sure she's going to want to talk to you, if that's OK with you."

"Sure, if it's OK with you. You know you don't need to be on the locked ward anymore."

"I like it here. I think everyone likes me. I help with the cleaning and stuff. I'm a volunteer taster for anyone who wants their food certified safe." He smiled. "I've found a home away from home. If you need the bed I'll move. Is that OK?"

"It's OK. I have to go now. I'll let you know when Elizabeth calls."

When Adam left Tom, he wondered who was getting more out of their meetings. Tom was giving him a tour of his trip through insanity, something Adam would never get from any book. Adam felt he wasn't doing much for Tom, almost exactly what he felt with Lillian. He thought, if he was still so fucked up, how in the world could he help anyone?

He took his time riding to Dr. G's. He wasn't too eager to talk about what he couldn't stomach about himself. He could still feel the rage simmering and had no idea what it was about. When he turned off the bike path he could see the old man at his station, feeding his pigeons. For the moment he was tempted to stop, visit with the old man, and blow-off his session. By the time he arrived at Dr. Goodman's office he wondered what he was going to talk about, effectively erasing everything that was bothering him. He realized he was late when he saw Dr. G's door open.

"Come on in Adam. I started to worry about you. You're usually right on time."

"What's the worry?"

"You remember what you were talking about yesterday?"

"Oh shit. I completely forgot until just this minute. I must be losing my mind."

"Or just protecting it."

Adam thought of Tom saying he was catatonic to stop from killing himself, as it all came flooding back.

"I was thinking of Lillian being violated...how enraged she was...wanting to kill the kids that raped her. I wasn't violated. I'm the violator, the killer. So what the hell am I so angry about?" He fell silent and his mind went blank.

"Tell me what thoughts and feelings you're having."

"What comes to mind is Tom. He's taking me on a tour of his psychosis. He's putting things together...explaining his actions...his symptoms. He's amazing, and here I am, his doctor, and I don't understand shit about myself." He looked at Dr. G and smiled. "I just thought of Tom coming into the ER covered with his own shit."

"In a way maybe that's what you're doing. Maybe there's a part of you that doesn't think you deserve to feel good. The black cloud you talk about. The pay-back for the blood you spilled."

"I think that's off the mark. It doesn't feel right to me."

"Well maybe I am off the mark. Let's see what comes to your mind."

"I don't know how in the hell this is related to any-thing but I thought of my mother and her being Jew-ish. That makes me Jewish. My father is Irish and was raised as a Catholic. He's a confirmed atheist but he converted to Judaism so that my mother could tell her family she was going to marry a Jew. He wanted to make it easier for mom and her family came around and accepted a "goyisher" Jew. My grandmother calls him her koshered Jewish son-in-law...I don't know why I'm talking about this."

"You haven't told me very much about your par-ents. I think they come to mind for some reason."

"I couldn't ask for better parents. I love them dearly and always knew they loved me. I thought about them a lot when I was in Korea. Wrote home often. It would make me laugh thinking about the heated arguments they would have about cases they were representing. I don't remember whether I ever told you they are law-yers. They met in law school. Did I ever tell you that?"

"Yes you did."

"I'm really proud of them. When they got out of law school they both became public defenders. Eventually they formed their own firm. My mom specializes in civil rights cases and takes pro bono cases from the ACLU. My dad does civil rights along with criminal defense work. He's defended some real sleaze balls. He says everyone deserves their day in court."

"Even you?"

That hit home. "You think that's why I thought of my parents? Like maybe I think I need a criminal defense attorney?"

"I don't think there's any maybe about it. I think you feel like a murderer for the people you killed in Korea ."

"I was in a war. It was kill or be killed. I slit that kid's throat to free Marines. I shot the wounded so they couldn't go for help or cut off our escape. What the fuck do you want from me?" Adam didn't realize he was shouting until he heard Dr. G's calm, quiet voice.

"It's really what the fuck do you want from yourself. You haven't been able to make peace with yourself. You've found yourself guilty and imposed a sentence that takes the edge off any joy that comes your way. It's a wonder that you've been able to allow Lillian into your life."

Adam didn't take his eyes off Dr. Goodman, looking for any clue as to what he was thinking about him. Adam knew he was really on the mark. He could feel the black cloud descending on him. He heard Dr. Goodman's voice as if it was coming from some other place.

"Adam, when you were late today and I told you that I was worried and you asked me what I was worried about. I was worried that you would find a way to hurt yourself. Ride off the bike path or something like that. I shouldn't have been surprised that you didn't remember what you told me in our last meeting. You've had to find ways to seal off the memory of what happened on that horrific day in Korea, or you probably wouldn't be where you are today."

The tears were rolling. Tears of remorse and relief. "I've always remembered what happened and what I did. I just disconnected the memory from any feelings I had about it."

"It's like your patient, Tom, becoming paralyzed, catatonic, protecting himself from himself."

"You don't think I'm suicidal, do you?"

"Are you?"

That stopped Adam. He started thinking about his binge drinking and his smoking like it was going out of style. He didn't want to talk about it anymore. He didn't like where it was leading.

"Tell me what you're thinking?"

"I'm thinking I don't want to talk about this anymore. I've had enough of Korea."

"Then why did you volunteer for another tour?"

"I told you I didn't want to talk about this anymore."

"You're going to have to talk about it if you want to have some peace in your life."

"Maybe I don't want peace. Leave me alone, goddamn it."

"There's a part of you that doesn't."

He wasn't smiling or laughing when he bolted for the door and slammed it so hard he thought it would come off the hinges. He was shaking with rage and sat on the curb until he calmed down enough to even think about getting on his bike. He rode over to the park where the pigeon nurturer hung out and just sat. He lost track of time as Goodman's words played back, over and over. "Why did you volunteer for another tour?" He thought of telling him, "I'm a Marine, stupid. That's where the action is," and then he realized that's how he felt then. Maybe he liked killing. He got medals and a promotion for it. He got on his bike and tried to blank out all of this shit. As he was nearing the hospital he thought he should call Goodman to see if he had broken his door, and for some reason that made him laugh.

Getting back to the hospital and making rounds was a great gift, a wonderful distraction. Sarah Johnston was out on the floor talking to one of the patients. When she saw Adam, she held up one finger which he took to mean that she would be with him in a minute, and not to leave until they talked. They were a good team. Adam wasn't looking forward to his next rotation and saying goodbye to her.

"Hi Adam." She gave him a once over, checking if he was all there. "The operator has been trying to get you. She's been paging you for the last hour."

"Oh. My pager must not be working." He smiled as he turned it on and it started to beep. He called the operator, apologized and told her the truth, his pager wasn't working. Tom's sister had called several times and asked Adam to call her. He called her back and when he told the receptionist who he was, she said Ms. Wittenbourne was expecting his call and she would be with him in a minute.

"Dr. Burns, this is Elizabeth Wittenbourne, Tom's sister. He said you would be expecting my call."

"Yes, he wanted me to talk with you. Tom is here under the name of Exxes, and I'm sitting in a nurse's station so I don't want to use your last name."

"I appreciate that, Elizabeth is fine. First, I want to thank you for taking care of Tom, he thinks you're the greatest. I've been so worried. I thought I had lost him." She took some time to compose herself. "How's he doing? He sounded like he was back to his old self."

For the next forty minutes Adam described Tom's progress from the night they first met to the clearing of his thinking once he started Lithium. Then Elizabeth told Adam about the onset of Tom's illness. She confirmed what Tom had said about the family and how he reacted to losing his brother.

"Tom has always been full of energy, he generates ideas at such a rate that oftentimes it's difficult to keep up with him. When Mark was killed, Tom went into a deep depression. He slept most of the time, moaning in his sleep. It was a sound of immense pain. I had to wake him and hand feed him. I thought he was going to die. You know, just shrivel up and fade away." There was a long silence. Adam thought he heard her crying. "I was scared to death he would die so I had him committed. He wouldn't go to the hospital voluntarily. He wouldn't talk. The doctors recommended shock therapy. I think he heard them talking about it because that very day he got out of bed and looked like he was getting back to normal, until he opened his mouth. His words came pouring out, it was difficult to make sense of them. The doctors called this loose associations, and they were loose. Senseless rhyming, talking to himself as if he were having a conversation with someone. He thought he was God's angel and he could rescue Mark from the ocean and bring him back to life. Then as suddenly as this craziness appeared his normal self would break through. This went on for almost eighteen months when one day he was gone. He walked out of the hospital and I didn't hear from him until today." Adam could hear her take a deep breath, almost a sigh of relief. "You know, I think Tom was scared to death of electric shock treatments. He knew I hadn't allowed it, but towards the time he ran away, I was starting to soften on it. I think even in his crazy state he sensed it, left and didn't call to tell me where he was."

"Now he can describe how his crazy thinking, as he calls it, gradually subsided and how our work together is helping him deal with losing Mark. But I have to tell you, I'm a first year psychiatric resident, so maybe you and Tom may want to see someone more experienced when he leaves the hospital."

"Dr. Burns, he's been at the most prestigious places in the country. You are the first who's been able to reach him, so whatever clicked between the two of you, it didn't have to do with experience. I look forward to meeting you." She was signaling that she had to go.

Adam came away feeling good about their conversation. He thought he would probably like her when he got to meet her. He had certainly heard of the Wittenbournes, but he purposely didn't do any research on the family. He wanted to hear what Tom wanted to tell him and experience Tom's family through his eyes, but he was curious as hell. He just got off the phone with a woman who sits at the helm of a business empire worth billions and she sounded pretty human. A lot like Tom.

After he finished seeing patients on his ward, talking with Sarah Johnston, he stopped at the locked ward to see Tom. He was sitting with one of the more regressed patients, helping him tie his shoes. Adam watched as he helped this infirm man to his feet and walked him to the day room. Tom was tender and radiating encouragement as he lowered him into a chair in front of the television.

"That was lovely Tom."

"That's what I've been trying to tell you...I'm a lovely guy." He laughed an appropriate laugh that just a few weeks ago would have broken the sound barrier.

"I just got off the phone with Elizabeth. For a CEO of a multimillion dollar enterprise she sounded like a regular human."

"She's more lovely than I am, and more modest. She's not the CEO, she's the chairman of the board. I'm the CEO." He saw Adam's look of surprise. "I didn't mean to shock you." He had second thoughts. "I guess I did mean to shock you. I love surprising people. I took the lead when I turned thirty-five, that's almost five years ago. Elizabeth was getting tired and wanted to spend her time with the foundation, and Mark was into his music and a recording company he was getting off the ground. Mark was quite a musician, a poet, a songwriter." Tom stopped, overtaken with such despair and grief, Adam wanted to scoop him up and comfort him. "Oh Adam, I miss him so. I'll never get over losing him." He gave way to a silent private grief, the kind that's so deep it doesn't see daylight and leaves a raw crater inside. Adam was tearing up in synch with Tom, and heard himself saying,

"There are some things we never get over."

Tom handed the tissue box to Adam. "I know there's also something you haven't gotten over. I truly feel for you, but selfishly I think that's why we connect.

You've been where I've been. Not as crazy, I hope, but enough to know me. I've been in some form of treatment on and off since I was six years old, but having a psychotic depression with swings into mania is very different. When I lost Mark, I lost part of my soul. It was like whatever connects us with ourselves, helps us feel whole and together, dissolved. It wasn't a matter of not being able to understand myself, it was a total shut down, like someone pulled the plug. I think the swings into mania saved my life. Crazy as a fruitcake but more fun."

Adam thought of his lost weekends wondering if they were anything like fits of mania. It didn't feel like it. It was an escape. What Tom was talking about was an attempt to preserve his life. Adam asked him if he was happy when he was manic.

"Happy? No. Tormented and twisted inside. Out of control. Like a rollercoaster that left the tracks. What is really scary is losing all moorings, soaring into empty space. But it's some relief from being in a deep dark hole."

Adam listened to this articulate man describe his insides and began to appreciate on a deeper level, the torment he lived through. He was in awe of his brilliance and felt so privileged to have him share this part of his life.

"Tom, do you know why you covered yourself with feces?"

"Boy, that was really crazy, wasn't it? I don't think I understand it all…I can't pass it off to a crazy man doing crazy things. I know that part of it was I felt like a shit-ball for not saving Mark. I know full well that most likely there was some mechanical failure. I would be lying on the bottom of the Atlantic with Mark and Dave, our company pilot, but just the same there's part of me that thinks I would have saved the day." He looked toward the heavens and made a grand gesture, then smiled, "I've always been a little grandiose and hypomanic but never off the charts like I have been these last eighteen months or so. I've been in analysis more times than I can count. Each time it has been enormously helpful but the shock of losing this dear soul I loved, did something to my brain. I'm sure of that. The Lithium put my brain back on track and you helped put my soul together. I'm certain of that also. I don't know how and I don't think you do either, perhaps between the two of us we can make — some sense out it."

"We can sure as hell try."

"I heard through the hospital grapevine you'll be rotating off the in-patient service. Will we be able to work together?"

"Sure. I'll be moving to the out-patient clinic and VA hospital. I want to work with you but I keep thinking that maybe you should be with someone with more experience."

"No. I need to be with someone who can first feel, connect and then we can put it together, together. I need to be with you, Adam. I love you. Call it transference, the missing brother, the wished for father, call it whatever you want. I know you're not gay. We will never have a sexual relationship, this need is not sexual. When in my craziness I told you I don't want to suck your cock, I was trying to tell you that, and it was so frustrating when you didn't understand. I think you got it now."

Adam laughed. "Yeah. I got it and I think now I'm getting you. When I first met you in the ER I knew you were terrified of something. When you told me your family was out to kill you it was obvious that covering yourself with shit wasn't going to stop a bullet. It sure kept people away."

"So you want me to analyze that?"

"Only if you think it would be helpful. Oh, that's bullshit. I'm also curious as hell, but I do think it will be helpful for you to know as much about you as we can." They both laughed at Adam's slip. "OK. I do want to know why. It was a pretty concrete way of saying how you felt about yourself but I'm finding it hard to get into your skin and understand what you were feeling."

Tom looked at Adam as if a light went on. "I think you hit on it. I didn't want anyone getting into my skin. Literally. I remember now how frightened I was that first night looking for a place to sleep. I didn't think this out but in my craziness I found a way to keep myself safe. I didn't sleep for days until I smeared myself with my own shit. It not only kept others away but kept me from getting close to anyone. I remember one night I went under this bridge to find some shelter. I heard this guy yell-out if I planned on spending the night I needed to get down wind from him." Tom started to laugh. "You should have seen the cops who brought me to the ER. They were gagging, holding their nose while trying to coax me out of the drain pipe I was hiding in. I think they were hoping I wouldn't come out. Then they didn't want to put me in their car so they called for an ambulance and dumped me on the paramedics. In my fit of mania I was deliriously happy over causing such a stink."

"It's kind of funny, but it also sounds like a lot of anger you were spreading around on everyone who touched you, or were trying to help you."   —

"Oh fuck you, Adam. You like raining on my parade? Haven't we done enough for today? We have to analyze, analyze, analyze, don't we? I've had enough for today."

Adam thought about giving him the line Dr. Goodman pulled on him and decided enough is enough. He smiled at Tom. "You're right, we've done enough for today, but I'll be back tomorrow." It was a Dr. Goodman type remark, delivered in a backhanded way and

Tom didn't think it was cute. Adam was reminded how angry he was at Goodman for keeping his nose on track. He would see Goodman tomorrow, but right then he didn't want to think about it. His thoughts went to Lillian.

■ ■ ■

16

Adam had a few hours to kill before Lillian was off. He thought about going to the ER just to be near her, but didn't think that would go over well. He started off to the resident's lounge, lost in thought, barely aware of where he was going. He felt like a star-struck teenager and was glad no one could read his mind, except maybe Tom. He was flooded with thoughts, talking to himself, half aloud.

"Tom would know I'm in love. So what? He knows what being in love is all about. He loved Mark and now he loves me…it's a little scary, I never thought I would ever need anyone. I didn't let anyone get close enough to really love…I'm a lot like that nurse at Bethesda who liked to fuck but any mention of love scared her so she'd freeze in the middle of an orgasm. I can't remember her name…Betsy something…Tauber…Betsy Tauber. The women I've made love with…wasn't love…maybe a kind of love of the moment. Sometimes love of a split second, it seemed like having an ice cream cone or cotton candy at the circus…So what am I so angry about?"

He was on the first step to the resident's lounge when his rational mind caught up to his scrambled thoughts. He heard himself saying, "This is what it's like to go nuts," then he nearly jumped out of his skin when he felt a pat on his back. It was Vic.

"Sorry I startled you. I think you were talking to someone and no one is here. You keep doing that and we'll have to commit you."

"So, you have to be careful who you sneak up on. You never know what could happen." He couldn't keep the edge out of his voice.

"Adam, you worry me. You're not a man at peace with himself. I hope you're getting help."

It was hard for Adam to restrain himself but he was able to damp it down a bit. "Now Victor, you know I'm the picture of mental health and I'm getting better everyday."

"I'm not judging you. I like you and I'm concerned for you."

"I appreciate that and I am seeing someone." He knew Vic was sincere and acting like the good chief resident. "I really do appreciate your concern. I've been seeing Dr. Goodman for almost a year and a half, and I'm in love. How about that?"

"Oh really. Who are you in love with?"

Adam started to laugh, the anger and tenseness dissipating. "Her name is Lillian Silver. She's the associate director of the ER. Do you know her?"

"I've only spoken to her on the phone. If you want my approval I'll have to do an intensive evaluation."

"OK. I'll tell her." Adam poured two cups of coffee and handed one to Vic. "I'm getting better. I'm a hell of a lot more mellow, even happy most of the time. I'm getting into some big time stuff that has to do with my military service, which I've taken great pains to avoid." He had never mentioned his service to Vic or anyone, and now he was inviting the inevitable questions. Vic didn't disappoint him.

"I heard you were in the service before med school, that's why you're so much older than the rest of us. I haven't heard it from you until now."

"You really know how to get to a guy. I'm not that much older than you."

"Maybe not in years, but it's pretty obvious you've aged beyond your years. The way you are with all of us, with your patients, and how no one, not even the chief of neurosurgery, intimidates you. It permeates the air around you. It's a quiet sense of strength and confidence some people get through experience and some never experience. I really admire you."

"Wow. I'm speechless. Thanks Vic. That means a lot to me."

"Well, this is a preview of the evaluation I'll be writing up. The other side of the coin is you need to stop cutting seminars and take more advantage of the faculty for supervision."

"You're right. I did read the articles you recommended. I was going to call one of the docs for supervision, but I was learning so much from Tom, I didn't want to get into theory. I thought it might interfere with my listening to him…I better leave now or I'll miss a seminar on psychopathology."

"Oh, so you're going to leave me hanging about your military service?"

"Next time. You wouldn't want me to cut class, would you?"

He left Vic smiling. Adam had no intention of going to the seminar and was about to leave the building when he had a sudden urge to masturbate. It came out of the blue. He hadn't jerked off since he met Lillian. He thought he was really losing control of himself and ended up going to the seminar as a way of cooling down so he wouldn't have to talk about it with Goodman. He felt like he was eleven or twelve and just discovered the joys of a forbidden pleasure. The seminar was more upsetting when the focus was on disorders of thinking, especially when the instructor described flight of ideas, which was what he was having about an hour ago. He thought he must be on the edge. He really didn't think he was crazy but started to think of psychosis in a different way. Maybe so-called normal people had bouts of craziness. The more attention he paid to the class discussion the less he felt the urge to masturbate and by the end of the seminar he completely forgot about it.

On the way to the ER he had to squeeze by Brenda Dobbs who was getting hit on by one of the residents. She was blushing, he wanted to tell her to relax and just let it happen. He was happy for her and hoped she really could just let it happen. He thought living in a self made cocoon was a terrible state of being. It made him think of the alcoholic cocoons he would lose himself in, that stopped him in his tracks. He stood still as if that would still his mind, then broke out in a sweat and found himself shivering like he was having a seizure. He nearly jumped out of his skin when someone asked if he was OK. It took him a second to respond.

"Yeah, thanks. I'm OK. I must be coming down with a cold or something." Actually he felt completely divorced from his insides and had a split-second squirt of terror. He had to stand off to look at himself, as if he was a detached observer. Only then could he move off the spot he was glued to. It was a new discovery. He just had an anxiety attack but except for that mini-second taste of terror, he didn't remember feeling anxious. He was beginning to get a handle on how flawed he felt, how fragile he could be if he let his guard down, even for a moment. It was becoming clearer why he's been so isolated, and had to shut out half the world. If he didn't he would be jumping at every loud noise and if he let another human being into his life, past the barrier of cordiality, he'd get flooded with all those he had lost and all the losses he caused others. He thought he could go completely mad, maybe he was on the threshold of knowing what madness is.

He was standing in front of the ER trying to snap out of it, determined not to let this craziness contaminate his love for Lillian, when he felt her arms around him and heard her whisper, "I love you Adam Burns." That's all it took to put the ghosts of his past back in the closet, at least for now.

———

They swam and had a light dinner at Lillian's. She was excited about her families visit and had the apartment set for their arrival, including a well stocked refrigerator and wine cooler. He was really proud of a beautiful navy blue blazer he found at the Goodwill store at the bargain price of two dollars and a red and blue striped tie for a quarter. It's the first jacket and tie he owned in a very long time and it would go well with tan chinos. He was all set for any fancy restaurant.

As Lillian talked about her family, her loving feelings were contagious, and he began to feel as if he knew them.

"My dad is a first generation American, the youngest of five children. His three brothers and sister are all alive and well with families of their own. It's a large family, and for the most part we get along pretty well.

Most of the time. Some of the in-laws are envious of Dad's success, and although he spreads the wealth around he's stuck to his guns about no family in our business. He says that once you start mixing business and family, you start losing your hair and any enjoyment from what you do."

"I have this picture of a man with a full head of hair, who enjoys life and I don't know what to call him."

"He does have a full head of hair, his name is Benjamin and he'll probably ask you to call him Ben. That is if he likes you." She laughed and started dishing out some ice cream she had set out on the counter to soften. "My mom is Esther and Emily is my sister, that's all I'm going to tell you. You'll meet them in a day and you can see for yourself."

"What if I don't like them?"

"You will. No doubt about that." She handed Adam a bowl of ice cream and fruit. "I've been waiting to tell you…I'm walking around unarmed. Yesterday I put my gun in the safe. I wanted to wait to see how I felt before I told you."

"So, how do you feel?"

"It's only one day, but I feel OK. In fact I didn't think about it much."

"Oh, Lillian, I'm so happy for you." He took her hand and kissed her.

"Let's not celebrate until I see if it lasts."

"Well you'll see how you feel day to day...this is a major step for you. We need to celebrate, besides it's fun to celebrate."

They ended up celebrating in the shower, on the bath rug, in the bed and love-making had really become making love. She was getting healthier. Adam was trying to catch up.

■ ■ ■

Adam found it easier to get going in the morning when he wasn't dreading the encounters of everyday life that most people don't give a second thought, but which push the danger buttons buried in the cement of his psyche. He hadn't been aware of living on hyperalert all these years, waiting for the sniper bullet, mortar round, jumping at sudden sounds or unexpected touches, but these last few months has brought the dangers of the world into sharper focus. He hadn't completely bought the company line, the more you know about yourself the better off you'll be, but he was limping in that direction.

He was thinking about Lillian and her being able to park her Glock semi-automatic. It was quite a leap into the world of reason. He was truly happy for her, a bit envious, but grateful she was blazing the way. He felt he was being pulled along with her, making it uncomfortable for him to lag behind. He didn't want to burden her and didn't want to lose her. Her voice brought him out of the cereal bowl.

"Adam remember that I'm getting off early to make sure the caterers are doing what they're suppose to, so come when you get off. My folks will probably be taking a nap but Emily may be up and around."

Adam's last words as they parted were, "I hope they like me." He drew a kiss and a pat.

He was a little early for morning rounds so he got to make the coffee. Vic arrived with Danish and Brenda, who looked like someone pumped a little life into her. Her hair was combed back in a pony tail revealing was her full face which usually is partially hidden behind a curtain of hair. She also had done some work on her eyebrows and eyelashes as well as a touch of lipstick. She's an attractive woman and was letting everyone see — no one was reluctant to tell her, much to her delight. They were a cohesive group, thrown together as rookies on a busy psych service. They drew strength from each other and an intimacy blossomed out of their anxieties. Brenda was flattered when someone suggested she must have gotten laid last night. Her non-committal smile left everyone to their own conclusions. Vic brought the group out of the camaraderie of jest to the camaraderie of learning. They listened to Eric Foster describe his encounter with an angry and distraught teenager who slashed her wrists. Vic engaged the group with some penetrating questions, which brought everyone into a collaborative learning process. This collaborative effort is palpable in the training program. It's part of what makes it difficult for Adam to decide whether he really wants to be a psychiatrist or whether he just found a safe warm home while he hopefully gets cured.

By the time rounds were over all the Danish was gone and the coffee pot was running on empty. Adam headed to the ward to make rounds and see Tom.

Tom was busy mopping the floor in the co-ed and only bath area. The wards in this ancient building weren't built for the mixing of the sexes. Staff and patients came up with ideas to be able to live together. The patients painted a sign with a Herculean male on one end, and a Marilyn Monroe look-a-like on the other, with an arrow on a swivel in between so everyone could see which sex was the current occupant. The occasional accidental intrusion didn't seem to be a big deal.

Tom looked up and smiled. "Hi Adam, I'll be with you in a few minutes."

When Adam stopped at the nurse's station he found Tom had initiated the formation of a patient committee which took over some of the chores on the ward. Every patient agreed to an assignment. There were helpers for patients who were not quite with it. It was a great push towards health and everyone wondered why no one had thought of it before. No one was anxious for Tom to leave.

"OK Adam. I'm sorry to keep you waiting but one of the stalls was in use and I had to wait for her to finish so I could clean the commode." He laughed. "How about that?" When they were alone he said, "This is amazing. Sophie, one of the most regressed patients, comes running into the bathroom, excuses herself, tells me she just couldn't wait and I should pretend she's not there. When she's finished peeing, she apologizes to me, returns to the day room and looks as regressed as ever. She had a moment of lucidity. There ought to be ways of stretching those moments."

"I think your idea of patients participating in their own care helps."

"Maybe it takes a person who's been there, to understand what's helpful. I'm learning a lot about myself and psychosis." Tom poured two glasses of water and handed one to Adam. "Do you want me to taste it first?"

"It's hard to tell whether you're poking fun at yourself or me. Maybe both."

"Both, I guess. This is the normal me. When Elizabeth gets here she'll vouch for that. I have a bit of a sarcastic wit, a teasing humor, but only toward people I love. I keep telling you, I love you. I don't think you really believe me. You think it's transference. I know it's real love. What's more I know you love me...what do you think of that?"

Adam started to laugh partly out of embarrassment, partly not knowing how to respond, most of all he thought this isn't how therapy is supposed to be. Then John Phillips popped into his mind, rather his head did — lying in his lap — detached from his body. He broke out in a sweat, trembling and heard Tom's voice.

"Adam, are you OK?" He was holding Adam. "It's OK. It's OK."

"Yeah. Give me a minute. I'll be OK. Thank you Tom."

They sat in silence, soothed by the quietness. Tom looked at Adam with love and concern. Adam knew he had to tell him the truth about what happened.

"Tom, this has never happened to me. When you were talking about loving me and my loving you, a horrific memory came flooding in.....I lost a close friend in the Korean War....I thought I had reached some semblance of peace about him...I have recurring memories of the war that seem to appear out of nowhere...I have no control over them."

"I knew there was something you were struggling with but wouldn't have guessed it was being in a war. So you've had your war and I've had mine. That's our connection. I was playing with soldiers and you were a soldier. I still have dreams of my war, disguised after all these years but I know them well...when I lost Mark they came back in waves that were intolerable to bear."

They sat together — with no sounds passing between them — a bond of knowing said it all. Adam thought Tom was right, "I did love him." Tom hugged Adam when he stood to leave.

"Adam, I watch you from the window in the day room and see you get on your bike when you leave. That's how I know you have someplace to go…in case you're wondering." They laughed. "Be careful on your ride."

———

Adam was smiling, being careful riding to Dr. Goodman. He wanted to check out his door — first thing — that's exactly what he did.

"My door survived, so did I, but next time try to tell me rather than showing me what *your* feeling."

you're

"So much has happened since I've been here I forgot why I ran out of here."

"You were pissed at me for pushing you."

"I don't remember what you were pushing me about, but I remember your pushing and I was getting angry…. sometimes it's hard to remember what happened here between sessions.….I think I thought…I….no….I didn't think I thought…I actually thought I was going crazy….I probably was crazy for a moment….longer than a moment …most of the day…I was having a flight of ideas and couldn't stop…it was like Tom, my patient. I remember…you were implying I thought I needed a lawyer and I was suicidal."

"I wasn't implying, I was telling you what I thought. I asked you why you volunteered for another tour in Korea."

When Adam spoke, he could feel the control in his voice. It came out stilted, like he was reading from a recruitment poster. "I was a Marine....a career Marine....that's where I needed to be...where the action is. If I was going to advance in rank I needed to command in combat. I went back as a company commander."

"How did you feel about going back?"

"I don't know...I didn't feel much....I think I had different feelings....on one hand I thought it was a phony war. We shouldn't have been there in the first place....but our guys were there and I should be there.....that's my job...that's bullshit. I wanted to go...couldn't wait to get back there but after a few months on the line I remember feeling what the hell are we doing here...why the hell am I here? I don't know what this has to do with it but you're always telling me to say whatever comes to mind. Yesterday Vic said I looked troubled and he was concerned about me. I told him I was seeing you and was getting better...working on some things to do with my military service. It was the first time I ever mentioned being in the military to anyone besides you and Lillian. I felt warm feelings towards Vic and when I left the room I started to feel crazy...that's when I couldn't control my thoughts…I felt I was having a flight of ideas…they made me dizzy. Out of nowhere I had this sudden urge to masturbate and hurried to the seminar I was going to skip, so I wouldn't. Then I wouldn't have to tell you about it…after the seminar I was walking in a fog over to the ER to meet Lillian. All these awful feelings went away when she put her arms around me and told me she loved me." He fell silent. After a minute or so which seemed like an hour, Dr. Goodman said,

"Love is very powerful. ~~You~~ your're loving Lillian and — ~~she~~ her loving you is making you both whole again."

"Oh I forgot, Lillian put her gun in the safe. She's no longer needing it. We celebrated and made love last night."

"That's wonderful and something to celebrate."

"Just before I came here I was with Tom. He poured me a glass of water, then asked if I wanted him to taste it first. We laughed, he told me he only teases people he loves. He loves me, knew I loved him and it wasn't transference…It was real…then John Phillips popped into my mind…I started to shake like I was having a seizure…scared the hell out of both of us. Tom jumped up and held me. When I recovered I had to tell Tom something. I couldn't leave him in the dark."

"What did you tell Tom?"

"I told him sometimes I have memories of the war that pop into my head and I have no control over it.

He was very understanding...he talked about both of us having our wars." Adam stopped talking. He was staring at his hands, laying limp in his lap.

"I have a feeling there's something you didn't tell Tom and now are not telling me."

"It's about John Phillips...I knew him from our days in Annapolis...we both were back on second tours...one night when we were drinking we decided to volunteer...he was a CO also...he was sitting next to me...we were looking at a map when a mortar round came in...the next thing I knew his head was in my lap...I'm looking at my best friend's head...not attached to anything...then there's a loud noise...the next thing I knew I'm in Bethesda Naval Hospital yelling something about this fucking war and getting a shot that put me to sleep for another few days." Adam didn't realize tears were running down his cheeks like a small waterfall until Dr. G handed him a box of tissues. He was into a deep silent cry and couldn't talk, couldn't move, until his internal clock told him it was time to leave.

Dr. G walked Adam to his bike. Adam turned, hugged him, Dr. G hugged him back. Adam walked his bike back to the hospital, feeling a soulful sorrow, long buried, lying beside a bed of rage at whoever sends young people to war. A part of him knew he was on the downside of his craziness, which helped with the pain, but he knew he couldn't keep John's head tucked away any longer or any of the other horrors sitting in his closet.

———

That evening he met Lillian's family. She was right, he did like them. He liked the way they treated each other and the way they accepted him — a little wary and protective of Lillian but trusting her to make the right choice. With one more, the Silver family could field their own basketball team. The women were six feet tall or close to it. Ben was at least three inches taller than Adam, which put him at six-six. Esther and Emily had the classic beauty that appealed to Adam. There were no Hollywood knock-outs in the Silver women.

During dinner Esther asked, "So where are you two in your relationship?" She was casual in her tone, but it sure wasn't a casual question. Lillian and Adam looked at each other and Lillian said, "You want to tackle that one, Adam?"

"OK. Where are we?" He spoke to Lillian, letting the Silvers eavesdrop. "We're in love and cherish each other. Our love is helping heal our wounds."

Lillian reached over, smoothed the scar over his eyebrow, and added, "Isn't that wonderful?"

Ben raised his glass. "I'll drink to that…Le-Chaim."

No one asked about their future. They seemed to understand exactly where they were with each other. There was no welcoming Adam to the family but there was a warm acceptance of someone who loved their Lillian. Later in the evening Ben and Adam were on the terrace, drinks in hand, appreciating the clear night and taking in the stars. Adam knew Ben wanted to say something. He gave him the room he needed. It didn't take long for Ben to find his way.

"Adam, I want you to know how relieved I am. I try not to be the over-protective father. I know I am...I try not to be over-bearing. Knowing you're such a positive in Lillian's life is a great gift to all of us." He took a sip of his drink. "I also want to be up-front with you. This may make you angry. I want you to know I'm not apologizing and I'd like you to hear me out." Adam nodded OK. "I did a background check on you. I know a lot about you, your parents, the schools you went to and your time in the Marines."

"So, how did I do? Did I pass?"

"Well tonight I realized I didn't have to do all that checking, so I guess this is an apology."

"I think we're even then. I had a background check on the Silver family from an inside source. It turns out she was right on." He admired his concern for Lillian, his being protective, didn't seem to cramp Lillian's style. He wanted his daughter safe. Adam was totally on board for that.

"I appreciate your being up front with me. You didn't have to tell me you checked me out."

"Yes I did."

They touched glasses and finished their drinks.

————

Lillian spent the next morning in a board meeting with the family while Adam took a bike ride on the path that paralleled the river. It was an overcast day, there was a mist rising over the river that gave it an eerie beauty best captured by artists and poets, making him wishful and envious of their talents. He was glad he passed up a lunch invitation from Esther and Ben, leaving them to be alone together, giving space to himself to just be. As he sat, mesmerized by the view, he was able to allow his thoughts free reign, and they brought him to Tom. He wondered what Tom would do once he left the hospital and hoped he would find a partner — a good person — someone that truly loved and valued him. He wanted Tom to have the same joy he found with Lillian. He thought of Tom telling him of his love and knew that he loved Tom. In a different way but perhaps not so different. He wondered how it would be living with, making love to and loving a man. He didn't feel sexually attracted to men, but he thought maybe he was kidding himself. He was very close to John Phillips, and he does love Dr. Goodman and Tom. He mused what if everyone was openly bisexual? Was the camaraderie in the

Marines a more acceptable form of homosexual love? That made him break-up in laughter. He looked around to see if anyone heard him. The Corps would rescind his medals and medical retirement. He tried to give his mind a rest, the thought of his next assignment to the VA intruded. He wasn't looking forward to working in the VA clinic, listening to veterans telling him war stories. That thought woke him from his reverie. It was getting late. Time to head back to Lillian's.

———

Dinner was at the Gourmet Room, a high priced restaurant on top of one of the skyscrapers. The maitre d' greeted Ben by name and Adam passed muster in his bargain blazer and tie. They had a wonderful dinner with superb food, warm laughter and good conversation. Lillian told them of Adam's Goodwill purchases. Adam showed off the expensive dark red lining of his blazer along with the previous owner's initials. Toward the end of dinner, after several glasses of wine, Esther, the perennial mom, couldn't contain herself and asked if they had ideas about getting married. Her speech was a little slurred and she was laughing when she caught herself.

"That just slipped out. I think I already asked you this. I guess I had a bit too much to drink or maybe just enough."

Lillian put her hand on Esther's arm.

At the end of the evening Adam said goodbye to the Silvers and went back to his place. He wanted to give Lillian more time with her family since they would be leaving the next day. He began to appreciate the enormous amount of love and support Lillian had to help her through the trauma of being raped. He could only imagine how a fifteen year old girl on the cusp of blossoming into womanhood might have felt being tossed into the trunk of a car like a sack of potatoes and repeatedly violated. What if she didn't have the family she had?

And then he thought, "What if I didn't have my mom and dad?" They sat at his bedside for more than two weeks while he was in a coma or whatever it was he was in. Sometimes he thought of it as more of a twilight zone. There were flashes of memory when he thought he heard them talking to him. They talked or read to him non-stop. They were the first people he saw when he woke up and opened his eyes. Adam remembered his mother's laugh when the first words out of his mouth were, "Where the fuck am I," followed by a long tirade about the fucking war. He remembered the look of concern whenever he tried to talk since his speech was punctuated with a fuck, shit or some other obscenity, accompanied by a wink or head-nod that was the icing on the cake. This went on for a month or so. The neurologist thought he had some form of tic douloureux caused by the head trauma. He had hopes of it resolving itself or with medication. Either his mother or father would be at his bedside during those days letting anyone who asked him a question, know what to expect. A one star general came by to present Adam with a purple heart. His father intercepted him, preparing him for what he might be the recipient of. The general thought with that kind of vocabulary Adam would make major in no time. At the time Adam didn't think it was very funny. He didn't remember whether he gave the general a parting fuck you.

He was on some sort of seizure meds when it suddenly subsided. He was eventually weaned off the meds. For months he held his breath hoping it was finally over. The loss of power to control what came out of his mouth accompanied by the winks and head-nods which accentuated the words was truly frightening. Every once in a while he would have an awful premonition it was all coming back. He thought he needed to tell Dr. G about this. He also needed to call his mom and dad to tell them he loved them and tell them about Lillian.

■ ■ ■

18

Tom had become an honorary member of the ward staff. It was obvious to all, he left his psychotic state *had* *n* and was firmly planted in the here and now. It was also clear that he would be able to leave the hospital whenever he chose. No one was in a hurry to see him leave, especially Sophie Day. Sophie and Tom had formed a special bond. She would sit, curled into a regressed state, in what looked like deep depression, until Tom came in with her food tray and hand-fed her. At first there was some rumblings from the staff about this budding relationship, but no one could deny that Sophie was getting better. Tom had become the sustaining force that was bringing her back to life.

Adam was late getting to the ward and Tom was finished with his chores. He was sitting in the day-room talking with Sophie. This woman who was so regressed just a few days ago was smiling, her hair was combed and she even had some lipstick on. She looked as if she came back to the land of the living. Tom asked

Sophie if Adam could join their conversation and he was about to introduce him when Adam said,

"You're Sophie Day. I've seen you perform. It was last year at the Hay Stack. You were wonderful. It was your last night…you were about to go on tour."

Adam couldn't believe this was the same woman. He never would have recognized her a few days ago. They talked for about an hour. Sophie did go on tour and word spread about her group. She was drawing big enough crowds to graduate from clubs to auditoriums and was gearing up for a Canadian tour, when she suddenly lost her husband of ten years. They were both recovering alcoholics who met at an AA meeting thirteen years ago, fell in love and eventually married. Her husband, Ned, played base guitar and was her manager. They had switched their addiction from alcohol to running and were dry for twelve years. When out for a morning run, Ned was hit by a drunken driver and died in her arms at the roadside. Sophie didn't turn to drink but fell off the cliff into a deep depression, stopped eating and slept most of the time. Her sister brought her to the hospital about the same time that Tom was admitted. In their state of almost total collapse they connected with each other. She watched Tom get better and for some reason this pulled her towards health. She thought Tom radiated curative vibes to her and to all the patients on the ward. He was sent on this mission by God. She added that she wasn't delusional but this is what she believes, and she was getting better so she could join this mission.

Adam didn't have enough time to meet with Tom, so he told him he'd come back to see him. Elizabeth was coming in today and Tom wanted Adam to meet her.

On his way to Dr. G, he remembered how much he enjoyed seeing Sophie perform. She sang country and blues with soul and great range. By the time he got to Dr. G, he was full of good cheer. He wanted to keep it that way. When he walked into the office, he sat with a silly smile on his face. Finally he said, "Did I tell you that Lillian is no longer packing?"

Dr. G smiled. "Yes you did."

He thought he would talk about the Silvers. Then Sophie and Tom took center stage. When Dr. Goodman asked him what was going through his mind he told him about Lillian's family, then his talk with Sophie Day. "Did you ever hear her sing?"

"Adam, do you remember what you were talking about in our last meeting?"

Adam looked bewildered.

"You told me about a horrific experience you had in Korea...what you're living through right now, is how you dealt with having your best friend's head in your lap. The memory of it is too much to bear so you've buried it."

It all came back. Except the feelings. "So what do you want me to do with it? I can't put his head back on." They sat looking at each other for quite a while. It was like who was going to blink first. "I remember what I was feeling last time. I was saved by the bell. It was time to leave…I felt like I was drowning…about to suffocate…I thought I would start to scream and would never stop." Adam started to fill up and stopped talking. He sat and looked at Dr. Goodman. It suddenly hit him that this was now or never. No one could make him face the horrors. He thought, "If I don't want to or can't…I'll have to live with…whatever…it's up to me….except I don't know what to do…how to get rid of the demons inside me…the horror of what I've seen…done." And that's what he said — everything he thought he said out loud and meant every word — he kept repeating over and over, the mantra, "the horror of what I've done." There were silent tears, reverent tears, for all that happened, all he had seen, all he had done and for John Phillips, who lost his head. He was turning the page — sad — glad — turning the page.

He biked back to the hospital feeling as if he had aged in the last hour. Maybe settled is more like it. Like a house settles on its foundation. More firm. Less cracking around the corners. Tom took one look at him and knew something was different. He couldn't quite put his finger on what it was but he said, "Adam, you look like you got something settled today." Then he smiled, "I'm glad for you."

"Thanks Tom. I'm learning how to live with the horrors of my war just like you've learned to live with the horrors of yours." He didn't think about whether this was OK to say in therapy. He knew it was OK to say it to Tom. Their relationship was changing or rather had changed.

He met Elizabeth and she thanked him for helping Tom. She thought Tom was back to where he's Tom again, and from what she said he functions at an extraordinarily high level. Although she said she has trouble keeping up with him, Adam didn't think she had that much of a problem. They talked for over three hours and it was evident in the first few minutes that these sibs were at the top of the charts when it came to brain power. They had grown a substantial inheritance into a multi-billion dollar enterprise, including a foundation that funded non-profit aid organizations world wide. Adam learned a lot about Tom that helped him understand some of his thinking when he was psychotic.

Elizabeth described how Tom would roll up into a fetal position, moaning over and over how he could have saved them. Most of the time he was talking about Mark and Dave, then his voice would change to that of a little boy and she would hear mumbles of mommy and daddy. He'd have brief periods of lucidity when he could connect with Elizabeth and amidst tears and sobs he would say he was a better pilot in an emergency and could have saved Mark and Dave. Adam learned that both Tom and Mark were licensed commercial pilots complete with certification in multi-engine jets. Adam asked Tom if he still thought he could have saved Mark and Dave.

"I'm not crazy anymore, at least not at the moment. What I do know is I have a capacity to process various kinds of data from multiple sources and decide on a response before most people realize what's happening. So if there was a problem on that flight that was correctable, I would have known what to do seconds or minutes before Mark or Dave. Would it have made a difference? I don't know but when I was in the depths of a psychotic depression I thought it would. The guilt I was feeling was real and unbearable." Tom took Elizabeth's hand.

"When I was brought to the Emergency Room I told Adam my family was out to kill me." He was still holding Elizabeth's hand as he turned toward Adam. "There's only two people in my family. Elizabeth wouldn't harm a hair on my head. So, in my craziness, I was asking you to protect me from me." He kissed Elizabeth's hand. "I was consumed with guilt...mixed with a sense of profound loss...judged by a hanging judge...sentenced to die for my sins...saved by a forgiving God...anointed with the holy bodily excrement of Jesus...all rolled into one brain that belonged to me." He stood, stretched and took a breath. "When I look back on the months my brain was out of whack...it's amazing to me…all my racing thoughts, paranoid delusions, flights into the body of Christ as well as Satan…it feels like a mosaic of an abstract painting … discordant music encoded into a psychotic sculpture of multiple meanings…hard to decipher… maybe we can work on it."

Adam was in awe and when he asked Elizabeth if this was Tom at his norm, she said,

"I don't want to embarrass Tom, but my dear brother is one of those rare human beings who's compassionate, insightful, empathic and completely unaffected by his genius. Yes, this is Tom. My lovely, loving Tom." She went on to tell Adam, how he grew their financial empire, is fluent and literate in Spanish, can hold his own in French and German, and among other talents is an accomplished violinist. She sounded like a proud mother rather than a sister and by the end of the three hours Adam had a picture, at least a snap shot, of how these three siblings survived and nurtured each other after the murder and suicide of their parents. Adam remembered Tom saying that he was glad his mother and father were dead and how Elizabeth and Mark were by far better parents. "The luckiest queer in the world."

Towards the end of the visit with Elizabeth and Tom, it was clear to Adam that Tom was getting ready to leave the hospital. As if on cue that's exactly what he said.

"I'm ready to give up my space on the ward. I would like a few days to say goodbye to everyone I've grown so fond of. I want Sophie to know I'm not leaving her. If you have a sudden influx of crazies and need the bed I can always move in with you." He smiled and looked at Elizabeth. "Are you ready to have me back?"

He really didn't have to ask.

■■■

Adam hadn't realized how attached he had become to the ward staff, until it was time to leave and start his rotation at the VA hospital. Until recently, getting close to people was not part of his repertoire. When Dr. Goodman told him people who have suffered traumatic losses or have lived through a war, often have trouble allowing themselves to get too attached to anyone, he didn't think it applied to him. It's amazing that John Phillips didn't pop into his mind when Dr. G said that. He buried John soon after he met with his parents. He buried his visit with John's parents along side John. There was no room in his head for his friend, the headless John Phillips.

Adam had lots of company at the Veterans Hospital. It seemed like an epidemic of symptoms of trauma. Some blatant and crippling and many more disguised in vague physical complaints which seemed at times more disabling. What he wasn't prepared for was the prevalent attitude that veterans have to prove they are

entitled to care and an assumption that most were looking for something for nothing. Shades of big Mike and
the mantra of the "Brick Tit", which was the unofficial
name of the VA Hospital. What big Mike said at the
poker game was the pernicious undercurrent that was
fouling the air, making it very difficult for Adam to
breathe. After a few weeks he decided every time he
heard belittling and disrespectful comments about a
veteran he wouldn't let it pass. He was going to find
someway to change the milieu, at least on the ward he
was assigned, as well as with anyone he had to interact
with in the clinics or ER. Vic thought he was on a quix-
otic quest but wished him well.

So it started with the first ward staff meeting when
Adam was introduced to Ira Stone. The staff knew and
were fond of Ira. He would manage to get admitted to
the psych ward whenever it was time for a disability
evaluation. On the surface there were good natured
jokes about Ira's checking into his private hotel, but
it was clearly implied that he was putting something
over on the system. Ira was assigned to Adam who got
the impression this was his initiation to the ward. Everyone was sitting arranged in a circle. There were two
vacant seats on either side of Ira, isolating him and
clearly creating an uneven playing field. No one had
mentioned he had lost his left leg just below the knee
in WWII. Adam sat next to him, turning his chair to
make eye contact.

"Mr. Stone, I'm Dr. Burns. I'm going to be your doctor."

He shot Adam a smile, revealing some missing teeth. "Glad to meet you Doc. You can call me Ira. I'm not used to the Mr. Stone bit."

"OK Ira. The nurses tell me that you check-in about this time every year. It sounds like the VA has become your home." Ira nodded and looked like he was expecting to be told the VA wasn't running a hotel. "I'd like to get to know you…if you mind talking in front of all these people, we can move to someplace more private."

Adam got another smile accompanied by a wink. "Depends on what you want to know, Doc. I'm not going to talk about anything intimate with this large audience unless I can charge admission."

There was laughter and perhaps some surprise at the way Ira expressed himself. As it turned out Ira started relating to Adam as if no one else was present. The first thing Adam asked was how he lost his leg, and Ira said, "I don't like to talk about that."

"OK, Ira. How about the headlines and not the details?"

He laughed, "I left my leg in a meadow in France. I'd been hit by machine gun fire which shattered my lower leg."

Adam tried to get beyond this flat toned account of his losing a limb and was the recipient of a menacing glance and tone to match.

"Hey Doc, I told you I didn't like talking about it."

"Yeah, I heard you didn't like talking about it, but that doesn't mean you can't."

Ira looked at Adam with disbelief, stood and walked behind his chair with his hands resting on the back. Adam didn't know whether he was going to pick it up and bash him in the head, so he stood and put one foot on the seat. Although Ira was small in stature, Adam could see well developed arm muscles flexing.

"You weren't going to smash me with the chair, were you Ira?"

He managed a smile. "The thought crossed my mind, Doc."

"Well I'm glad it was just a thought." Adam took his foot off the chair. "Ira, I've read through your chart. I've got some ideas of what's bugging you all these years. If you want to try and reclaim your life you're going to have to talk about what you've been through." Ira didn't take his eyes off Adam. His face was frozen with no signs Adam could read to have some clue as to what he might be thinking. So Adam decided he was not going to patronize this man or treat him like a child.

"Think it over, Ira. If you want to work with me let me know before four o'clock. That's when I leave for the day."

Ira cracked a smile. "What if I can't decide by then?"

"If I don't hear from you before four, forget it."

Ira Stone left. Adam wouldn't take bets on what he would decide. When Adam asked the staff what's next on the agenda he took some heat for what he said to Ira. To say Adam was surprised by some of the comments would be an understatement. There was great concern Ira would file a complaint with the Veterans' Rep for being refused treatment. There was no questioning of Adam's motives for saying what he did, or why Ira would be reluctant to talk about his experiences. Most felt Ira didn't want to talk about how he lost his leg because he had been asked the same questions over and over for the last fifteen or more years and nothing changes for him. Adam asked if anyone had any ideas of why Ira would cling to a vagabond existence, following the weather, migrating from one VA hospital to the next? He got a range of thoughts with the common denominators of, he's too damaged to be able to change and he doesn't want to lose his 100% disabled status. When Ira didn't hunt Adam down before four o'clock, Adam started to think maybe they were right.

In the next few weeks Adam met a few more Ira Stones. He began to realize there were a good number of chronic patients who were frozen in time. They saw no hope in being able to change their lives and their only life line was their disability payment. If they got better their disability payment would be reduced. He started obsessing about this system that rewarded people to stay sick, and he wasn't too quiet about it. He thought Ira Stone lost his leg and shouldn't have to go through a re-evaluation every year. He got into it with Vic at rounds pretty regularly. Everyone was getting tired of hearing about Ira Stone. Bob Hansen said he had enough of Ira and the rest were unanimously in agreement.

"OK…this guy lost his fucking leg and it's not going to grow back so why the fuck does he have to grovel for a god damn disability check. Why not give him a permanent pension and tell him he earned it…then ask him if there is anything else we can do for him…maybe if he believed the VA was on his side and wanted the best for him…maybe..just maybe it would help him get a life for himself."

Vic said, "I agree with you about the system but the ward staff on psych, and most of the other services, are dedicated people. They give good care within this much to be desired system…they give it their best shot…by-the-way Adam, Ira Stone has gotten a life for himself."

Adam wanted to argue with Vic. He didn't like being told to shut up. As much as he didn't want to admit it, Vic made sense and it did shut him up for the moment. He still wanted to fight but didn't know who to get into it with. After rounds Adam sought Ira out.

"Hey, Ira, I thought for sure, you wouldn't be able to resist working with me. You really hurt my feelings."

Ira smiled. "Don't take it personally Doc. I'm not up for talking about the war."

"Yeah, I got the message. Can I be of help in any way?"

Ira gave Adam a long appraising look, and said, " Doc, it would be of great help to me if you didn't fuck up my disability rating."

" The only way I would do that is if I could grow you another leg."

As they started having coffee together, the ice between them began to thaw. They didn't decide they would have coffee together, it just happened. Ira would tell Adam little bits about his war, the war that was still going on in his head. Adam knew from his chart he was with the 82nd Airborne, but didn't know he lost his leg on a daylight air drop where his unit were sitting ducks for enemy fire. Ira still had dreams of that day, but they are more disguised ~~slept~~ and he most often ~~sleeps~~ through them. He ~~has~~ most had of the other symptoms of post trauma, the most crippling, a chronic anxiety. For a couple of years he drank heavily but it didn't help his anxiety ~~so~~ he smoke, cut back on alcohol. He still ~~smokes like it's~~ going it was out of style. One day he looked at Adam and smiled,

"I don't know why but I think you've been through some of what I've been through."

Adam thought of Tom Wittenbourne, and wondered what signals he ~~gives~~ off.

gave

"Yeah I have, Ira. How did you know?"

"I don't know. After awhile I begin to sense when I'm with someone who's been in combat. Some of these guys have never been shot at. I can tell when I hear stories that aren't the real deal." He refilled their coffee cups. "Don't get me wrong...they're as fucked up as any of us...just being around a war is enough...take Gus over there." He pointed to a grey-headed guy with a full white beard who was sitting in a rocker talking to himself. "Gus was an airplane mechanic...he has the guilt of the war on his shoulders for all the people his airplanes bombed." He flashed a wry smile at Adam, who could guess what was coming. "So what's your story, Doc?"

Adam tried to give him the same hard look Ira had given him. "I don't like to talk about it, Ira."

"Touché Doc...then how about the headlines? We could go someplace more private." They were both laughing as he replayed their first meeting.

"I was in Korea. My right femur was shattered...they were able to save my leg with a lot of hardware to patch the bone together."

There was a cunning smile, serving notice that it was still Adam's turn to talk. "I gave you bigger headlines than you're giving me. Are you going to even things out?"

"I don't know exactly how it happened but they tell me it was a mortar round. I was unconscious for about three weeks…when I woke up I was in Bethesda Naval Hospital with my mother and father on either side of me…I thought the war was over. I didn't know then, it's never over."

"Yeah, it's never quite over."

They sat in silence drinking their coffee. Adam was wondering why he told Ira as much as he did when Ira said, "If you were in Bethesda you were either a Navy corpsman or a Marine…I'll bet corpsman, that's why you became a doc."

"You'd lose the bet. I think we're even now Ira. Let's turn the page on war stories."

And so they did, but Ira wanted to talk or maybe needed to talk. They kept having coffee and after swearing Adam to secrecy he gradually told him what his life has been since he left the Army. Adam didn't have to take an oath, Ira's story was the kind most people wouldn't believe anyway. He just wanted to make sure none of what he shared ended up in his VA hospital chart, because he sure as hell would lose his disability rating.

Ira was in his first year at Vanderbilt when Pearl Harbor was hit. He was seventeen, on an academic scholarship majoring in English. He tried to enlist but he needed parental consent. He didn't know where his mother was and never knew his father. He was raised by his maternal grandparents and lived with them in Nashville. They insisted that he at least finish his first year of college. They thought he would be more apt to finish college when the war was over if he had one year behind him. They were partly right.

When Ira hit eighteen he enlisted and volunteered for airborne. Throughout his entire tour he kept a diary in which he wrote everyday. He also wrote long letters to his grandparents. He wrote poems, short stories along with stories about guys in his unit — about death and killing — about how he was changing inside. By the time he returned to Nashville, his grandfather had died, and his grandmother, who was as feisty as ever, was determined to get him back in college. Partly to pacify her but mostly because he loved her, he enrolled in Vanderbilt with a major in creative writing, booze, smoking weed and having an affair with one of his instructors. His grandmother died — he never finished college — his instructor became his life-long lover, editor and literary agent. Ira's poetry has been published in several prestigious literary magazines. He's written three novels which have been well received. His first, about his war, was enough of a commercial success so his royalties dwarfed his disability pension. All his work is written under a pseudonym which he didn't share with Adam.

So everything has gone well for Ira, except the low level of anxiety which has become part of his constant background noise. It erupts about twice a year to levels that drive him to the VA.

Adam asked, why is it so important to have a 100% disability rating. He certainly didn't need the money and in fact donates it to several veteran organizations. Ira took a swig of coffee and a long draw on his cigarette, and said,

"I don't know why except it's owed me. I need to know the VA is here for me. When I feel like I'm jumping out of my skin it's like my anchor. It will always be here."

Ira's main anchor is his love, Julie. He didn't mean to call her name, it slipped out one day when he was telling Adam how she handles all his business dealings. He's proposed to her many times and she tells him she always wants to be with him but if they married it would ruin their relationship. Over the years, he's pleaded with her to change her mind, but deep down he knows she's right. So they worked out an arrangement where they own everything together, each having power of attorney for the other. They just are not officially married. When Adam asked why he thought it was a better way than being married, he said,

"Doc, the trouble with all you shrinks is your always asking why…why this…why that. If you have to know the hidden meaning of everything you do…every book you read…every movie you see…it takes the joy out of living. Julie and I have found a way to beat the devil. We live up a storm most of the time…makes it easier to live with the left-overs…most of the time."

It was just a few days later Ira told Adam he was ready to leave. He had his artificial limb refitted, his teeth fixed, his anxiety under control and his 100% disability intact. Adam walked him to the street where they shook hands and he grabbed a cab to the airport. A few weeks after he left, Adam received a package posted from Puerto Rico. It was a book, "The Last Assault," by I. Piedra. Inside there was an inscription, "don't analyze – just enjoy" and signed, "mucho gracias, I. Piedra". Adam guessed the book was from Ira but he wondered why he thanked him in Spanish. It was Vic who knew Piedra was Spanish for stone.

■ ■ ■

20

"**L**illian and I have been together for almost ten months...I can't believe it...I've never been with anyone so long...our love seems to grow stronger each day...yet she never mentions marriage and when I do we both come to the same end. It feels like it's better to leave things as they are, like Ira. We love each other...don't want to be away from each other. There's something about getting married, we think may ruin what we have. We don't want to chance it...I don't want to chance it...I don't want to think about living without Lillian."

Dr. Goodman looked like he was in a pensive trance. Adam didn't think he was going to respond, when he said,

"I've been thinking about you and Lillian and the concern you have about getting married, like Ira and Julie. I've heard these same fears many times. I think it may be too close to home. Maybe that's why I haven't been very helpful in getting to the roots of it. Remember, I've also been exposed to the horrors of war."

He spoke in a measured caring way with unmistakable humility. He was admitting his own problems might interfere with his being able to help Adam with his. Adam's first thought was Dr. G was telling him he may have to see someone else. As this flashed through his mind, he felt as if his insides were being ripped out. He couldn't catch his breath — couldn't speak and broke out in a sweat.

Dr. Goodman was on his feet, "Adam, are you OK?"

He couldn't answer but nodded, "Yeah…give me a minute."

It took more than a minute before Adam could tell him what he was feeling at the thought of losing him.

"I thought my hands were bloody…I saw John Phillip's head in my lap. I knew it was somehow connected to my fear of getting married…the fear of losing you…I felt like I was being turned inside out…It's like floating above all that's happening without being connected, nobody knowing where I am…Having no feelings. Just numb."

"This is how you can be immune to feeling, even the kind of terror that's paralyzing. You can be somewhere and not be there. I think that's how you were able to survive two tours in Korea, but *you're* starting to allow those feelings to emerge a bit at a time."

"I remember guys freezing-up in a shoot-out. They were so paralyzed they never fired their weapon. Maybe for a few minutes or the next day they were over it. It took some reassurance…not that they wouldn't get killed but that freezing-up happens…that never happened to me. I never felt scared. It's hard to believe but I can't remember ever being frightened…maybe because for the two tours I was there I wasn't there…now that scares me…it feels so unreal now to think of being so cut off from my insides for so long. The most horrible thing that ever happened to me was looking down and holding John Phillips head in my hands and I didn't or don't remember feeling anything. Maybe I wasn't in a coma for three weeks but just didn't want to wake up and feel anything……..I think my first step back on earth since the war was when I fell in love with Lillian. Now I feel there's no me without her. I don't think you think that's the picture of health and maybe I don't either, but I know that's how it is."

Adam fell silent — the kind of silence that says do not disturb and Goodman read the sign. A few minutes passed, then Adam continued where he left off, as if no time had elapsed.

"Some of the veterans at the VA seem to be there and not really be there. Maybe I'm projecting what I'm learning about me, on to them. I guess they'll let me know if I'm not on track."

"Well Adam, that's a good way to test out your take on things as long as you can let yourself hear what you may not want to hear."

Adam was starting to get pissed, but was learning to take a step back and listen to what he was feeling.

He knew Dr. G used a teasing tone but he wasn't going to give in right then, so he smiled and told Goodman he hadn't heard a word he said.

Dr. G smiled back. "I said it's time to stop."

———

Adam thought it was time to stop not being, but found it hard to let go of his protective armor which had been so effective, especially when most people didn't realize he really was not there. He spent the rest of the rotation at the VA making a concerted effort of being there. He found it was exhausting, when he could allow himself to step from behind the shield of a half-involved observer. He also became aware of how professional helpers are able to come to work every day and still maintain some semblance of sanity, along with a life outside the help giving arena. They all seem to relate from positions of relative detachment. Some more detached than others. He had everyone under the microscope, cataloging degrees of their capacity to be there and began commenting on his findings at morning rounds.

Once more, he was trying the patience of his fellow residents, as all the patients he saw, all the instructors, staff and faculty had their turn under his scrutinizing eye. He finally put a lid on it and focused on trying to help veterans deal with their insides. He started an out-patient group for veterans who were plagued with the classical symptoms of trauma. He didn't know how much help they were getting from meeting once a week but it seemed being together had some healing effect. It was rare anyone missed a meeting.

One day a former Navy corpsman joined the group. He sat down and started talking right off the bat. This was unusual for a first timer, but as it turned out he was pleasantly stoned. He was a face full of smiles while blips of tears made spot appearances, as he told his story.

"I'm Larry Owens. I just retired from the Navy six and a half months ago. I had thirty years in and retired as a Chief Petty Officer so I'm on a pretty good pension. At 48 I should be sitting pretty, but ever since I left active duty I've been thinking of blowing my brains out. I don't know why...all I know is I can't get out of this hole I'm in." All the time Larry was talking his smile never wavered. It was frozen in place. It seemed like Larry was in deep freeze. He sat there with his smile as he was peppered with questions. Finally he said,

"I hear ya all...but I don't know what to say...I have to tell you I've been smoking pot this morning...in fact I smoke most of the day...tried booze but it makes me sick and I spend the day vomiting...weed is the only thing that helps...if I try to sleep my dreams wake me up and my wife tells me I'm screaming something about hold on I'm coming, I'm coming, over and over like I was back in Korea and that's what it feels like…like I can't get to everyone who needs me." Someone said it must be hard for him to now be the one who needs help. He was still smiling but needing help was the last thing he wanted to hear.

Every time Larry would stop talking he would sit and stare at Adam with the frozen smile in place, while the questions or reassuring comments went on. It was like he had to take a breather or the weed was putting him on hold for a moment. His stare turned into a hard look-over and he said,

"Doc, I know you from somewhere. I've been trying to figure out where I've seen you. Your name sounds familiar…Do you know me?"

"Not that I know of Larry."

He was scratching his shaven head when he burst out with, "I know, you look just like this guy I had in intensive care for about three weeks who was in a coma. I'll never forget him. He had closed head trauma, lost half a lung and had a busted up femur they were trying to patch together. His mom and dad never left his bedside and when he woke up one day he had one of the most foul mouths I've heard. He couldn't stop himself. Every other word was shit or fuck."

"Oh shit, fuck, Larry, that guy is me."

Well that broke the ice for Larry. The group jelled around hearing of Adam's tic douloureux. Perhaps more about learning that Adam shared some of what they've been through. After a week or two they wanted to meet more often, and started meeting on their own. Larry found a purpose in life after the Navy, as everyone started looking to him as the doc. He needed to be needed.

They were an amazing group who were available to each other twenty-four seven, much like a group of AA sponsors. Adam started meeting with Larry outside of the group meetings. Larry eventually felt at ease telling Adam about the time he spent in coma and the enormous amount of care his parents gave him. He told Adam how they moved him, massaged him and made sure there were no pressure points or bed sores. They talked and read to him non-stop. Adam knew they had been there for him, but to hear it from an eyewitness opened a new depth of appreciation and love for his mom and dad, which made whatever gratitude he had shown them pale in this new light.

———

Adam's time at the VA was coming to an end as was his first year of training. He had to turn in a list of preferences for the second year and he still had reservations about becoming a psychiatrist. His obsessing about, to be or not to be, was getting on Lillian's nerves, as well as his own. One day she had enough.

"Adam, I think you should take a leave of absence."

That's all she said. No reasons or heady thoughts about it. Adam gave her a quizzical look. He was about to ask her why she thought he should take a leave, when she said,

"If you ask me why I said what I did, I'm going to bop you on the head. Just do it. If you're so goddamn ambivalent about continuing in the program it's sure as hell a good idea to take a time out." She waited. Adam didn't say a word. They stared at each other until Adam started to laugh. "You're right...so right."

She gave him a hug, "Oh Adam, you really scared me for a minute. I was about to call for the straight jacket and have you locked up."

Obsessive thinking tends to hang around and in Adam's case it helped him procrastinate sending Dr. Martin a request for a leave of absence. Dr. Goodman also got a dose of tortuous listening which he didn't put up with for very long.

"Adam, it's time to get off the pot. When you do, it will be easier to understand what you're holding on to, what's paralyzing you."

He wrote the letter and Dr. G was right, it was easier to see how he didn't want to let go of this comforting place. He knew that being a psychiatrist was not a good fit for him but he didn't want to leave the psychiatry residency. It was the most nurturing, stimulating, growth promoting experience he ever had. He wasn't looking forward to telling the man who created this gift of learning, he wasn't going to continue.

He hand-carried the letter to Dr. Martin's office and was greeted by his secretary, Mrs. Beaman, "What a coincidence, I was just about to call you. Dr. Martin would like to meet with you."

He handed the letter to her — smiling — and said, "If it's about what I've written in this letter I'll know for sure that Dr. Martin can read minds."

"No, Dr. Burns, I haven't mastered that feat yet, but there must be something to mental telepathy." He had just come into the office and overheard what Adam said. "I just got a letter from Elizabeth and Thomas Wittenbourne, I need to share with you. Do you have a moment now?"

They exchanged letters and Adam was blown away by Tom's offer. Adam hoped that Tom wasn't into a manic phase of his illness. There was no hint of it in his letter but his offer was so generous that Adam couldn't help but wonder. Adam was relieved to see Elizabeth, as president of their foundation, had signed off on the proposal. They were offering to finance a psychiatric pavilion built to Dr. Martin's specification, with Adam's approval, to be named the Mark Wittenbourne Pavilion. The only requirement was the University had to provide a site Dr. Martin and Adam approved of. Adam's built in capacity to focus on what needed to be addressed, leaving feelings in suspension, kicked in and without any reluctance he said,

"That's a generous proposal Elizabeth and Tom have made. Have you had time to think about how you would like to respond?"

Dr. Martin smiled and, in his usual polite-formal-intimate style, asked if he could call Adam by his first name. Adam looked at this man, short in stature and enormous in good will, and wanted to sit in his lap and tell him he could call him whatever he wanted.

"If it's alright with you, Adam, I'd like to talk about your letter first. All your supervisors are quite pleased with your progress and think you will be a fine psychiatrist. Two of them said you were a natural, so I'm surprised you want to take a leave. Your letter gives me no hint to why, and I'm hoping you would like to share some of your thoughts...I'll understand if you don't want to, and of course you can have a leave of absence."

"It's a long story Dr. Martin. How much time do you have?"

"As much time as you need."

Adam felt as if he was part of Dr. Martin's extended family and knew he was asking out of a genuine inter-est and concern.

"Dr. Martin, I love being one of your residents, that's why it's so difficult to leave." He took a deep breath. "I'm not going to go into the gory details but I've been living with the horrors of two tours of combat in Korea for far too long...I've been in therapy with Dr. Goodman and I'm finally stepping out from under the black cloud that's been hovering over me...I now have a loving relationship with a women I love...I'm happy and hopeful for the first time in years." He stopped. Gathered himself and smiled through misty eyes. "Your training program has been a safe haven...nurturing, caring and challenging, but I've come to realize that being a psychiatrist is not a good fit...I have a need to get out and touch people and make a concrete difference in their lives. I don't know exactly how or what...I know it has something to do with the lives I took in Korea...the losses...the horror...I know I'll never be able to undo what I did, but I'm feeling better about myself. I'm going to continue to work with Dr. Goodman for a while but I think I'm ready to take a leave from him also."

Dr. Martin was leaning forward with his elbows on the desk propping up his chin, as he listened. His eyes were misty, in synch with Adam and there was no doubt he got what Adam was saying and feeling.

"That's quite a story you just shared. I'll keep it between you and me. I'm so happy you're feeling better. Of course you can have a leave of absence and if you ever want to come back you'll be most welcome. I hate to lose you but I have a feeling this will be a good move for you. Perhaps you and I will be working together on this Wittenbourne proposal." He gave Adam time to collect himself while he poured two cups of coffee. He handed Adam a cup and asked, "Do you feel up to talking about this most generous offer? It's almost too good to be true."

Adam took the cup he offered. "Oh it's a bona fide offer and they can make it happen if you're interested in following up on it."

"I certainly am. I had something like this in mind for a while but didn't know exactly who to approach or how I would get the funding. Can you tell me about the Wittenbournes?"

"Tom is in his late thirties and extremely bright and gifted...maybe in the genius category. His sister, Elizabeth, is not far behind. Tom is the CEO of the Wittenbourne empire. Elizabeth is chair of the board and president of their foundation. I don't think this is a public company; these two are it, as far as I know. Mark Wittenbourne was the middle child and was killed in a plane crash."

"Of course I know the name. There's a Wittenbourne museum and some chairs at a university...I've forgotten where. How do you know them, Adam?"

"I first met Tom, and then Elizabeth. I'll let them fill you in on the details of how we met. I would suggest you meet with them and perhaps get the University to commit the land first." Adam was no longer boy-resident. He had shifted into an equal partner mode and Dr. Martin picked up on it.

"I'm going to set up a meeting with the chancellor and I'll call the Wittenbournes. I think you should be at both meetings. Is that OK with you?"

"Yes, I think it would be important for me to be at the meeting with the Wittenbournes, and if you think I should attend the meeting with the chancellor, I certainly will."

Adam left Dr. Martin's office feeling he just started on a new career path without the slightest idea of what it was or where it would lead.

■ ■ ■

Lillian was on the phone when Adam got to the ER, still in her scrubs and signing "I'll be with you in a moment." She looked excited and as lovely as she always does to his eyes. He was sitting on a stool at the receptionist's counter when he heard a voice that sent his adrenalin flowing.

"I'm looking for Lillian Silver."

He was about five feet away from Adam — dressed in jeans and a wind-breaker type jacket. Adam was looking at a tattoo of the head of a snake winding up his neck, partly covered by long blond hair, when he shouted, "Where's Lillian Silver? I know she's here."

Lillian was moving toward the front desk, as he was pulling a semi-automatic from his jacket, shouting, "Where's Lillian...." He voice was cut short when Adam sprang from the stool — yelling at the top of his lungs — locking one hand on the gun and sending a chop to the head of the snake with all the inner force he could muster. There were two explosions — the sound ricocheted off the walls as the shooter crumbled to the floor. Adam stood holding the hot barrel of the gun and watched him twitch on the ground. He heard Lillian shouting,

"Adam's been shot in the abdomen — get an IV going — cross match for four units and alert the trauma team — let's get him to the OR — Stat."

As Adam was being wheeled to the OR he saw another team working on the guy with the gun. He was still alive. He remembered thinking he must be losing his touch just before the lights went out.

————

The trauma surgeons worked on Adam for six hours, resecting a section of damaged large intestine, repairing one of the larger mesenteric arteries and cleaning out his abdominal cavity. He was lying in intensive care with an IV antibiotic drip going along with some morphine. His eyes struggled open, one at a time, and he thought he glimpsed Lillian before the curtain came down again. She stood vigil for several more hours until Adam regained consciousness and appeared to be in the present — once more.

Lillian was bending over him, smiling, wiping and caressing his forehead. "Well my dear you gave up part of your large intestine for me."

"I've already given you my heart so why not have all of me...I'll even put that to music especially for you." He felt the pain when he started to laugh, but it felt good to laugh with Lillian. It felt good to be with her. "I love you...the last time I was in intensive care I was unconscious so my luck is improving. I'm not only awake, you're here alive and well."

Lillian bent close to kiss Adam and he whispered, "I meant to kill him."

"I know Adam...I know."

She then told Adam they were still working on the guy. The neurosurgeons had decompressed his spinal cord and he started to get some feeling back in his extremities.

"He's Edward Bennett, the guy that tried to assault me fourteen years ago, and threatened me when he was sentenced. He's been out on parole for about a month."

Before Adam made the national news, Lillian called his parents to let them know what happened and that he was OK. His doctors and nurses held off the press but he had to give a report to the police. He told the detectives that he knew this man was a danger to everyone in the ER, but when he specifically asked where Lillian was, he snapped. He told them he had little memory of what actually happened but knew he had to stop him before he hurt Lillian. When Adam told them Lillian is the woman he loved and was in love with, they smiled, and wished him well before they left.

Adam was in the hospital for more than a week, hooked to an IV antibiotic drip for an on again off again fever. He had more visitors than a new mother. Dr. Goodman and Dr. Martin visited. Tom called to wish him well. He gave Adam his private number in case he just wanted to talk, but he still called every day. One day Adam awoke from a nap to find Tom sitting by his bed, holding his hand. He was as pleased to see Tom as Tom was to see him. They talked until Adam started to fade out — smiling as he drifted off.

Adam wasn't prepared for the outpouring of concern from his resident group who kept bringing him milk shakes and ice cream and giving him hell for leaving the program. They all got to meet his parents who didn't waste anytime getting to his bedside. When Larry Owens came one afternoon, Adam's mother instantly recognized him. Everything came flooding back on her. She cried, his Dad cried, Larry the caregiver, comforted them, and Adam slipped back into being there and not being there. The past came to life for him once more. To make sure it stayed alive some enterprising reporter dug up Adam's service record and wrote an article about a Korean War hero who saved the life of his loved one. The story was picked up nationally. Adam started to get requests for interviews, asking if he would be interested in running for office, making a movie or selling his image to advertise everything from soap to guns.

Adam felt as if his cover was blown and he was totally exposed. He hid out at Lillian's place and she insisted his folks stay in the guest apartment. Adam felt a little strange to hear her talking to Rebecca and James, using their first names, and hearing her laugh at some of the family stories. They got along well and Adam knew they liked each other. Adam was getting stronger which allowed them to consider getting back to work. It was after dinner on the night before they were to leave when Adam told them what Larry Owens said about them.

"He said you never left me alone…there was always one of you there…talking to me, reading to me, washing me, turning me, loving me…It was so different hearing someone describe what you both did when I was out of it…I've never told you how much I love you both and how lucky I feel having you as parents, so better late than never." He filled everyone's glass and toasted them. "To my Mom and Dad…my love, my thanks." He felt awkward as the words came out of his mouth but he was all there and full of love for them.

———

Adam had a few days left in the residency program. He wanted to say goodbye to the staff and the veterans group. He had been doing some mild work outs at Lillian's and thought a walk to the VA would be a piece of cake. It took a lot more effort than he imagined. He was reminded of the first long walk after they pinned his leg for the third time, minus the pain and fear it might give out.

The first person he ran into at the VA was big Mike. He was getting out of his car as Adam came up the walk. Mike stopped and asked Adam how he was doing.

"I'm getting my strength back and feeling pretty good. Thanks for the card you and the Poker group sent. I appreciate it."

"I want to apologize for my behavior at our last game. I now understand why you were so pissed at me. I deserved it."

"I could have made my point in a gentler way rather than disrupting the whole evening. Let's call it even."

When they shook hands he felt Mike's strong grip, and realized he had a lot more to do to get back in shape. He also needed to find another Poker game. By the time he made the rounds to say goodbye he was ready for a nap. It was good to see the guys in the vets' group and he was pleased to hear Larry Owens had been hired by the VA as out-patient group coordinator. Larry was back on track and had three groups going — working on a fourth. Adam was drawing lots of complements. He was feeling like a celebrity — a very tired one. When he got back to Lillian's, he called Dr. Goodman, made an appointment, then with beer in hand fell asleep on the chaise on the deck.

Adam didn't hear Lillian come in but her fragrance found its way into his dreams and her kiss welcomed him awake. He knew he had killing field dreams — their remnants slipped away and left him in a cold sweat.

"I thought you were burning up with fever but you're ice cold." She got a warm wet cloth and started caressing his face and whatever part of him she could see. "The horrors must have had a curtain call...I bet your new wound has opened some old ones." She fell silent and Adam knew she was struggling with something when she said, "Adam, I know I shouldn't have done this, but I went to see Ed Bennett. He's still in ICU with a cop on guard. He's totally immobilized on a Stryker frame. He didn't recognize me so I told him who I was, and he just stared at me...didn't say a word. I asked him why he hates me...why he couldn't let it go...he just gave me a silent stare. Finally, I told him it feels like he's forgetting he was the one who broke into my room and tried to rape me. If I can stop hating him, he ought to be able to stop hating me. I thought his facial expression softened a bit. I wished him well and told him I hoped he'd have a quick recovery."

Adam sat up and held her close. "I wish I could feel that way. I would like myself better. Does it look like he'll recover?"

"I ran into your favorite neurosurgeon who said it's too early to tell, but he does have some feeling and movement in his feet, so he may get back more function."

"See, I gave Dr. Rademyer a case to operate on after all. So we're even now." Adam took a sip of warm beer. "I hope seeing Bennett brought you some feeling of closure. You're more gracious to him than he deserves. I hope you aren't thinking of a return visit."

She smiled and went off to heat up some soup that Sarah Johnston sent over. Adam wasn't thrilled by the smile.

■■■

Adam was still in his shorts, making breakfast for Lillian. He was thinking about a lunch meeting with Tom before they were to meet with Dr. Martin, when her breath on his neck sent all those thoughts to the back burner. They kissed.

"What were you thinking besides not over-doing the eggs?"

"I was waiting to be caressed by my love, thinking about why Tom wanted to meet with me first, before our meeting with Dr. Martin." Adam flipped the eggs to their plates, added bacon and toast and poured the coffee.

Lillian smiled. "I like your taking care of me and love watching you flip those eggs."

"Since I'm unemployed I have to earn my keep, besides I love taking care of you. Which reminds me, I wanted to ask you about your visit to see Bennett."

"What do you want to know?"

"I guess what I really want to know is how you can stop hating him, when I still want to finish him off?"

"I don't have an answer...I don't know why I don't hate him...I don't know why I went to see him but I think it has to do with my being able to be at peace with myself. I think I'll try and see him again...maybe it will help him as well as me...I don't know."

Adam wanted to tell her not to see him again but knew she may have to. He reached over and kissed her. "You always amaze me."

"Well the amazing Lillian has to go to work. I'll leave you with the dishes since you're unemployed."

————

Adam was feeling good about Lillian, as he slowly biked to Dr. Goodman's. He was not feeling so hot about himself. It had been a while since he saw Dr. G and a lot had happened. Adam didn't know what to talk about first. He could hear Dr. Goodman saying, just say what comes to mind, that's exactly what he said.

"It's about Lillian...no it's about me...she went to visit this guy who tried to kill her and he seems to be recovering some feeling in his legs and she asks him why he hates her and tells him that he was the one who tried to rape her and if she doesn't hate him why can't he get over his hatred and I'm listening to her thinking if I visited this guy it would be to finish the job and I'm thinking she's a wonder and I'm a cold blooded killer because the only reason he's still alive is that I didn't have good footing to take him out and that's what's on my mind." Adam waited — catching his breath. Goodman didn't say anything.

"Didn't you hear what I said?...When he was yelling for Lillian and pulled the gun I didn't think I'm going to kill this guy...It was instinct...I wasn't trying to subdue him I was going to kill him...no thought no hesitation just kill him...like crushing a roach or swatting a mosquito...the only thought I had as they were wheeling me to the OR and I saw he was still alive is that I was losing my touch." Adam sat, exhausted, waiting for him to say something. "I'm getting offers to make a movie, book contracts...make commercials...the next thing you know I'll be on the Wheatees box...a celebrity...killer of the year...pretty funny." He sat in silence and all of a sudden everything he said started to sound ridiculous and he found himself smiling and suppressing a laugh. Dr. Goodman caught the smile.

"What are you smiling about? Something strike you funny?"

"I don't know...all of a sudden my ranting feels ludicrous...like I just made a commercial or something."

"What are you selling, Adam?"

Adam was smiling, barely able to contain himself. "That I'm a cold blooded killer."

Dr. G looked intense, serious, he wasn't smiling. "I'm not buying it. I don't think you are either. If you were cold blooded about the people you killed and the killing you've been part of you wouldn't be sitting here. There wouldn't be any black clouds hovering over you."

"Well I don't feel any guilt about wanting to kill this guy or even wanting him dead now. How do you explain that?"

"So if you went to see him now, you would kill him?"

"No, but I sure as hell wouldn't forgive him like Lillian did. I'd tell him if he ever came near her again I'd finish the job."

"Well that tells me, you and Lillian are unique and separate individuals. She feels differently about this guy than you do, at least at this point in time. You love her very much…you know better than I do what she would do if the situation was reversed, if this guy was going to kill you and she could do something to stop him…she put him in the hospital once didn't she?"

"OK Dr. Goodman, so protecting someone you love is different than killing innocent people." Adam was choking up and couldn't continue talking. He was silent — sitting quietly — the tears slowly making their way down his cheeks as the sorrow that was buried began to seep to the surface — the children and their mothers and fathers and grandmothers and grandfathers that he walked around and over — the helpless wounded all came flooding back along with John Phillips's head — only on this time around there were no filters — a potpourri of guilt — sorrow — anger — flowed over him like lava from a slowly erupting volcano — both agonizingly-painful while offering the promise of peace at long last. They both sat quietly and when it was time to go he told Dr. Goodman he was going to be alright — he was finally getting right with himself.

Adam wondered how many times does he have to relive the past in order to let it go. Maybe it's never ending, but it's becoming less of a power in the way he felt. Each time he's been able to get a hold of his insides he comes out with a slightly altered view of his life — of the utter madness of war and how easy it is to meld into the madness — and it's terrifying but sobering — and before he knew it he was at his apartment into the world of the living, and thinking he was going to have to buy some more clothes to live out of his apartment as well as Lillian's.

————

He felt smug in his two dollar blazer and twenty-five cent tie, walking into the ritzy hotel where Tom was staying. Tom met him at the front of the main dining room with a warm smile and handshake to match. He had gained back his weight, looked strong and weathered as if he had been working outdoors. Tom radiates a vital energy which is commanding and intriguing. It fuels the curiosity he has about people and their lives. It is part of the appeal he has that goes beyond looks and makes him someone you want to know.

The maitre d' ushered them to a secluded table he'd reserved for Tom.

"Well Adam, I would have had lunch served in my suite and given you a big hug but I didn't want to throw you into a homosexual panic…but I still love you."

"Thanks Tom. It's good to be with you again although this place is a real come down after the psych ward…you look well and healthy…what have you been up to?"

"I just got back from Africa, where I spent most of the time outdoors with a conglomerate of foundations, who are working to come up with a unified effort to control malaria. I've also been working on solar power and accessible water projects. Let's order lunch and I'll tell you why I wanted to meet with you before our meeting with Dr. Martin."

Tom was all there in his thinking, with no signs of mania. He is seeing a psychiatrist who is helping him wean himself from Lithium. He talked about his work with enthusiasm and clarity, in a way that Adam knew Tom had resumed the reins of being a CEO.

He was finishing his salad and took a sip of wine when he told Adam why he wanted this meeting.

"Since you're no longer my shrink and are unemployed, I want to offer you a job. Before you tell me that it may not be ethical for you to work for a former patient let me just say, bull shit. I've read about twenty articles on transference, boundaries between former patients and their docs and I can tell you that I know where I start and leave off and I think you do also. If you accept this job and it doesn't work for you, you'll quit. If it doesn't work for me I'll ask you to quit or fire you if you don't quit. I will always love you. I know you are not my brother or my idealized father or mother and I know you're not perfect, but I see qualities in you that makes me think you would be a good fit for the job I have in mind."

"So my friend, who is not saddled with a blinding transference and only loves me because I'm so lovable, what do you have in mind?"

"I was thinking of a position of project manager. I'm looking for someone to oversee the foundations projects in our social and health programs. You have the background I'm looking for."

"Oh Tom, I don't have any experience in business or running companies and there are plenty of smart people with MBA's out there...besides loving me, why me?"

"While liking and loving the people that work for me is the most important consideration, I don't run a multi-billion dollar enterprise based solely on good feelings. I've researched your background and you have exactly the qualifications I'm looking for. If you didn't we wouldn't be having this conversation."

"OK, so what qualifications do I have that you're looking for?"

"You probably have forgotten your calculus and engineering courses you had at Annapolis, but I'm sure you'll be able to understand an engineer or architect and know what questions to ask...your medical training is a major plus and you know how to deal with people...you're not afraid to take command when the situation demands it...I hope you're taking all this down...you can use it in a résumé in case you don't work out with me." Tom finished his wine. "If you're still reluctant, why not take on this psych pavilion project and see if you think this sort of work suits you. It will also give us a chance to see if we can manage our hot transferences."

Between Ben Silver and Tom's background searches, the article in the news, Adam felt totally exposed but was feeling good about not being described as a cold blooded killer. He told Tom that his offer did excite him and the psych pavilion project would be a good test of how they could work together.

"I'm glad Adam...so let's settle on a salary. The usual initial salary is 50,000 plus health benefits and expenses. If you decide to stay on we can renegotiate. Is that OK with you?"

"I don't know Tom, that's only 46,800 more than I made as a resident and I had my meals thrown in, but I think I can get by on it."

Tom was blown away. He couldn't believe that someone could live on 3200 a year. He told Adam how wonderful it felt to rescue him from the depths of poverty. He assured him, he would earn every penny of his salary. They spent the rest of the time talking about some of the problems Adam might run into dealing with the University. When Adam said he didn't think there should be any problem giving a university a free building, Tom smiled, and said, "Adam, you're going to learn a lot on this project."

They moved to a small room that was part of Tom's suite. It was set up with a tray of assorted desserts, coffee, tea and enough different soft drinks to satisfy anyone's taste or desire. It was Adam's first lesson. The holder of the purse strings can set the stage and make the call where any meetings would take place. Tom did not want to meet at the psych pavilion where he is also known as Tom Exxes.

Adam thought Tom and Dr. Martin would be comfortable with each other but could not have predicted how instantaneously they hit it off. Within a few minutes it was Maury and Tom talking as if they were old friends, and Maury was well prepared for the meeting. He had given a lot of thought to the purpose and function of a behavioral science center which he thought would be the important determining factor in the ultimate design and size of the building. Adam listened to Dr. Martin talk, as he watched Tom take it all in and ask thoughtful questions. Adam remembered Tom saying that he would learn a lot on this project and earn every penny of his salary.

Tom smiled at Maury, "You've been planning this center for awhile, waiting for the opportunity to make it a reality." He offered Dr. Martin and Adam drinks and sat back with a bottle of juice. "We'll need some engineering and architectural input but off the top of my head I think we'll need about 100,000 square feet. We are probably looking at a three to four million dollar project. I'll run all this by Elizabeth but I think our foundation will take it on." Adam was evaluating Tom as he spoke and was brought back to the moment when he heard Tom say,

"Elizabeth and I think Adam has all the qualifications to oversee the healthcare and social initiatives that our foundation is involved in. He wasn't sure he wanted to make such a radical change. I don't think it is such a radical change but I'm not Adam. At any rate he's agreed to oversee this project and see if it fits with his future plans. I'll be in contact with Adam, but he will be representing the Wittenbourne Foundation."

Tom stood to signal the end of the meeting.

"Maury, you're a lovely man. It's a real pleasure to meet you. I can see why this is such a sought after training center. I know if my brother were alive he would feel the same. I'm pleased we can contribute something to help make your dream a reality."

After Dr. Martin left Adam waited for Tom to ask how he felt and when he didn't it was another reminder that he was making the leap from the world of psych case conferences to the world of business deals. Tom was focused on the project.

"I think one of your tasks will be acting as the hard nosed buffer between Maury and the University administrators. Maurice Martin is a lovely man, but he has to live with the administration and you don't...remember, you have the authority to kill this deal...move it off campus...privatize it...the administration needs to know if they get too greedy or overbearing that's exactly what you'll do."

"It sounds like you're talking from first hand experience of giving money to universities. I can imagine having difficulties if there were some crazy demands tied to the gift, but giving them a building, I can't believe there will be problems."

"Well we'll see...come, I want you to say hi to someone."

Tom led the way into the living area of the suite where Sophie Day sat at a desk, busily taking notes and talking on the phone. Her hair was bright red, curling down over her shoulders, adding contrast to a turquoise blouse which was tucked into tight-fitting black silk slacks. She was striking and looked as Adam remembered her on stage. When she hung up, he gave her a hug.

"You look wonderful Sophie. What a come back."

She bowed. "Thanks, Dr. Burns, great to be back, in every way."

"Everyone calls me Adam. It's so good to see you...Tom what a surprise...are you two an item?"

"Tom and I are living together. I love this man who has helped me come back into this world but he is unseducible, though I'm working on it."

"Sophie and I have been together since she left our beloved ward. She just finished a recording on Mark's label. She's trying to convert me, at least to the bisexual world. I keep telling her I'm not wired that way but it's wonderful being with her. As I told you, there's all kinds of ways to love." He kissed Sophie and she more than returned the kiss. "Sophie has a gig tonight. We would like you and your partner to join us for dinner and her show."

"I'd love to. I'll check with Lillian to see if she can join us."

"OK, I look forward to meeting Lillian...a beautiful name. Let's meet here at six so we have time enough before Sophie's show."

Adam left feeling he had stepped out of a frame of the past and taken a step into the future.

■ ■ ■

Lillian was delighted to dine out, meet Tom and especially Sophie. "I'm going to have dinner with Sophie Day. I have her recordings, she's amazing. How about that?"

"You're also going with a rich handsome guy as your escort. I'm no longer unemployed. How about that?"

He told Lillian about his meeting with Tom, the arrangement they came to about working for his foundation and managing the behavioral science project. "We're going to give ourselves time to see if my working for Tom is doable, if it is, he wants me to oversee the foundation's social and healthcare programs. I had some concerns about our relationship...my working for a former patient...it's not considered the thing to do in my former profession, so Tom suggested this project be the test...so that's what it will be...if it's not working for me I'll quit...if it's not working for him he will fire me."

"Congratulations my rich friend. How rich are you? I may want to make a loan."

"During this trial period I'll only be making fifteen and a half times what I was paid as a resident…I had to give a lot of thought to whether I could make ~~due~~ on 50,000 rather than 3200 a year. Tom was blown away when I told him what a resident's salary was."

They talked, rested and resisted the urge to blow off Tom and Sophie and make love. It was a hard sell but they managed to drag themselves to the shower to cool off. Adam was ready first, all decked out in what he wore to the meeting with Tom and Dr. Martin. There are advantages to a limited wardrobe. He watched his lovely Lillian put on a touch of eye shadow, and he was amused thinking of Tom telling him how he hugged this fat assed nurse. Now Tom was entrusting him with a 4 million dollar project. Adam had the sobering thought maybe Tom had lost his mind or maybe he was losing his. He replayed today's meeting — Tom wasn't manic — no flight of ideas — a little full of himself but not grandiose or off the charts.

"Adam, come back from wherever you are. We need to get going."

Lillian was wearing a black sheath with those thin spaghetti like straps, thin gold choker necklace and small gold stud earrings. She had a darker red lipstick and more eye liner and shadow than usual. Adam had never seen her like this. "You take my breath away. Will my kiss smear your lipstick?"

"It's the no smear kind, we can test it out."

And so they did.

Tom and Sophie met them at the front desk. Tom took one look at Lillian and said, "Oh my god. Will you ever forgive me?"

Adam wouldn't have taken bets he would have recognized Lillian or even remember how he greeted her.

She gave him a hug. "Now we're even."

He turned to Sophie. "I told Adam I gave this fat ass nurse a hug and now I realize I was totally out of my mind. Your ass is wonderfully proportional to your beautiful body. I'm so embarrassed. Adam, you gave me no warning and now you know when people are psychotic they still have a memory…at least this psychotic does."

"If we're finished discussing my ass I want to tell Sophie how thrilled I am to meet her. I love your music."

Tom led the way to the café where they'd have dinner and where Sophie would perform. He was greeted by the maitre d' who reserved a secluded table, with a good view of the stage. Tom told Sophie about his first encounter with Adam. He not only remembered everything, he was totally accurate. Sophie chimed in and told Lillian when she first met Tom and Adam. She was sitting mute in the corner of the ward sucking her thumb. She also had total recall of how she was and how people related to her. They both talked of their trip into the world of the crazies as if they were describing a long overdue vacation from the real world where they could regain their strength to live again.

At dinner the focus was on Lillian. She needed no prompting to share her excitement over her plans for the ER. Adam's eyes were on Tom, who listened, asked sensitive and often penetrating questions, and whose laughter had no sign of that maniacal ring. He was charmingly appropriate and engaging, as was Sophie. No one would have guessed just a few months ago, Tom was caked with his own excrement and Sophie was curled into a fetal ball. They were waiting for coffee and desert when Tom said,

"Adam, I think you've been sizing me up all evening like you're not quite sure I'm back to normal. Is that right?"

"I'm wondering what in the world am I doing agreeing to run a 4 million dollar project…are you in your right mind to even consider me for this job…are you crazy or am I…or maybe we both are."

"I know I have the family history that goes with a diagnosis of manic-depression. Maybe that's what I've got…right now I'm back to how I've been for most of my adult life…as for you, my young friend, you'll get over your doubts about yourself when you see how good you are at the job and get past those rules about re-lationships with a former patient. I'd like you to call Elizabeth, and ask her why she thought you are exactly the person we are looking for." Tom took a sip of the newly arrived coffee and fed a taste of the chocolate con-coction he ordered to Sophie. He lifted his class and pronounced, "The most potent curative agent of all is love…your love…my love…our love…true and quite profound."

The vote was unanimous, love was indeed all it was cracked up to be.

Adam watched Tom kiss Sophie and offer her an-other taste of chocolate before she left to change for her show. Tom's eyes followed her as she walked back stage and when she disappeared behind the curtain he said,

"I love Sophie…she still mourns Ned and I still mourn Mark…we help each other…we're growing more and more together."

Lillian took Adam's hand and Tom smiled, "I'd bet you two know what I'm talking about."

They were finishing desert and the waiter was top-ping off wine glasses when Lillian suddenly noticed the room, which must hold a couple hundred people, was over-flowing. She looked at Tom,

"Where did all these people come from?"

"It's show time and Sophie packs them in. The combo she put together is terrific. You're in for a real treat."

The lights dimmed and they were looking at Sophie in an iridescent green blouse, enhancing her flaming red hair, and heard, "Let's give a warm welcome to Sophie Day." It set off a round of applause and signaled the combo to kick in with a rendition of, *Dancing Cheek to Cheek*, at a foot tapping tempo allowing this five foot three woman to show her range and her soul. For the next hour she played with her combo and the crowd, singing old favorites in the voice of classical jazz, soul, with a bit of country thrown in. When the crowd wouldn't let her go she sang, *At Last*, in a style reminiscent of Etta James. There was no mistake that she was singing to her love, Tom. She took two more curtain calls, shared the bows with each member of her combo and the crowd recognizing she had given her all, reluctantly let her go.

Lillian, leading the applause with her bravos, took Tom's hand, "She is a real treat. What a gift she has. Thank you for sharing her with us."

They went back stage to see Sophie who was resting, feet up and holding a glass of ice chips. "Come on in…have some ice chips…that's all I have." She looked at Lillian. "Well Lillian, are you still a fan? Did I do OK?"

"You were superb, Sophie. You can sing anything. I love the way you can move from soul, to blues, to any style you feel. I'm your fan for life."

Sophie was delighted and told Adam, "Take Lillian home since she's the one that has to get up early. I want to look after my best fan."

Adam said he would make sure she got her rest. "And what about you, Sophie... You must be exhausted."

"I need to rest my voice between shows. The rest of me is still raring to go." She took a sip of ice water. "I've got two more days here then I'm on the road again. Maybe we can get together before I leave. If not I have a feeling this is just the beginning for the four of us."

———

They decided to walk from the hotel to Lillian's, holding hands and feeling close in their silent walk. Lillian squeezed Adam's hand and said, "I vividly remember when the paramedics and police brought Tom to the ER... and now... what... seven months later he's transformed into a high functioning loving guy. It's incredible."

"You should have seen Sophie. She was in the same shape as Tom... both suffered overwhelming losses. Tom describes feeling as if all the circuits were blown and rearranged into an unmanageable network. Sophie looked like she totally shut down." They stopped and kissed. "I think we both know how they helped each other heal their wounds."

That night Lillian and Adam loved each other. The kind of love making that is slow, cherishing and soothes the way to sleep.

———

Adam was on hold, waiting for Elizabeth Wittenbourne to pick up on his call. He was trying out different ways of asking her if her brother was totally sane, when she clicked on with,

"Hello Adam. Tom told me you would call to find out if he was in his right mind and if I approved the offer he made you. The answer is yes to both."

"I also wanted to ask you what you see in me that makes you think I'm the one to oversee the foundation's projects?"

"Tom and I sign off on all major decisions. You're a major decision." Adam was waiting for more of an explanation. All he got was silence at the other end.

"Are you still there, Elizabeth?"

She laughed, "Don't worry. You will do well...now say thank you Elizabeth, and goodbye." That's what he did.

———

Over the next few weeks Adam had several long meetings with Dr. Martin. They were able to transform his dreams of a behavioral science center to paper. At least a rough draft. Adam asked Dr. Martin if he was ready to present the project to the University.

"I'm ready, Adam. I'll call the chancellor and set up a meeting. I'd be pleased if you called me Maury."

"That will take some time but I'll try."

It wasn't but a few days when he was walking with the good Doctor across campus to the chancellor's office, still wrestling with himself about calling him Maury.

The administration building was of the same vintage as the psych pavilion but it had been restored to it's original luster and eased into the twentieth century. A sign protruded from the wall marking The Office of the Chancellor. On a clouded glass window, in an antique wood door, the name, Aubrey B. Lowell, MD, MPH — Chancellor, was emblazoned in gold letters.

Adam could feel the adrenalin flowing, not quite pumping, the kind of excitement brewing when he would be gearing up for some action. It was like when he took command of his first company. It was not a bad comparison. He found himself slipping into a position of observant detachment, while being fully engaged. Maybe surveying the field like an NFL quarterback, making decisions while being part of the decision. He liked the feeling.

They were greeted by a pleasant matronly woman, who said she would alert Dr. Lowell they were here. A few minutes went by and no Dr. Lowell. Adam started looking at old photos of the campus that lined the walls. He spotted one of the psych pavilion taken back at the turn of the century. It was a majestic building that looked a lot better without all the air conditioner units protruding from it. By the time he finished the tour of the old campus ten minutes had passed — still no Dr. Lowell.

He gave the secretary a gracious smile, read her name on the desk plaque, and in a quiet assertive voice said, "Ms. McCabe, would you please let Dr. Lowell know I have another appointment after this. If much more time goes by we're going to have to reschedule." As if on cue, Dr. Lowell made his appearance showering them with the kind of charm Adam could do without. He was a sandy haired man of medium height, who looked fit and would have been attractive except for the stepped up volume of his voice and big toothy smile.

"Ah, Maury, good to see you...this must be our Adam Burns."

Adam managed to mutter something and took his hand. They followed him into his office where he introduced them to Jim Trundle, a VP of the University, and Bill Gordon, a consulting architect. He once more referred to Adam as, "our Adam Burns." Without losing a beat he began to layout some of the plans he had Bill Gordon draw up which included a place in the basement for nuclear medicine. Adam couldn't believe this man. He either had no idea of how he came across or didn't give a damn how he impacted people.

Adam interrupted. "Aubrey, if we're to work together on this project, I need to clear the air...first, I'm not your Adam Burns. I'm the project manager for The Wittenbourne Foundation...second...if you were offering to build me a four million dollar building, I wouldn't keep you waiting more than thirty seconds and third, most importantly, Mr. Wittenbourne is offering to fund a building to be named after his deceased brother to be called, The Mark Wittenbourne Center for the Behavioral Sciences...to be built to Dr. Martin's specifications and needs, subject to my approval. The offer does not include nuclear medicine or any other service. All of this is contingent on the University donating a suitable site and agreeing to maintain the building after it's built. This is absolutely non-negotiable." There was silence in the room and Adam let it sit.

Lowell regained his composure. "Adam, I don't know if I can justify donating the land unless there is some space allotted to other services."

"Perhaps you need some time to think it over and consult with your colleagues because that would be a deal breaker." Adam was thinking that it wouldn't look so good for him to lose this gift. He thought it would be good timing to end the meeting and let him stew for awhile. He was betting Lowell would try to talk to Tom directly when he popped up with,

"Would you mind if I talked to Mr. Wittenbourne directly?"

"No, that would be fine with me. He's going to be out of the country in three days so call soon or you'll miss him. Aubrey, if we're to meet again, I would like some representative from the board of directors present so we don't have to repeat these meetings and can get moving on this project. So why don't you let me know where the University stands on this by the end of next week."

They shook hands all around and Adam walked Dr. Martin back to his office.

"Well Dr. Martin, do you still want me to call you Maury?"

"More than ever, Adam. Aubrey Lowell is a bully with a large amount of rampant narcissism. You spelled out the conditions of the gift in a way that will avoid endless meetings, wrestling for who is going to be in the driver's seat. I enjoyed your comment about his keeping us waiting and you talked to him in a way that I would not have since I have to deal with him on lots of different issues."

"I hope he realizes I wasn't playing with him...what I said is not just a tactic in a negotiation. Tom told me to pull the plug on this project if we ran into someone like Aubrey. We can always build it outside of the University and have it under the auspices of your department."

"Knowing Aubrey, he'll call Tom, to charm him into submission...if he fails maybe he'll come to his senses. I hope so. I really don't want to lose this opportunity. I'm also curious why Tom chose our department. Do you know why?"

"I think I know some of the reasons but I rather you ask Tom directly. I thought you were going to do that when you met him. I was surprised you didn't."

He smiled, with a bit of tease in his tone, as he said, "I was going to but I had this intuitive flash it wasn't the right time...besides I thought you would tell me."

■ ■ ■

24

Adam left Dr. Martin at the steps of the psych pavilion and wandered over to the ER. He felt good about the meeting with Aubrey Lowell, now, he didn't know what he was going to do the rest of the day. He was used to having a full day with everything on a schedule, back to back appointments, and here he was with time on his hands, getting paid fifteen times what he made when he was working his ass off. He hoped Lillian could take a break so they could spend a few minutes together, maybe more than a few. She was at the front desk, smiling, as he came through the automatic doors.

"Do you have time for a break?"

There was some hesitation as if she was giving his offer some thought. When she collected herself she said, "I was just leaving to visit Ed Bennett. Would you come with me?"

The first reaction Adam had was a burning sensation in the palm of his left hand as he remembered grabbing the gun as it went off.

"I don't know...what would I say to the guy...sorry I messed up and didn't put you out of your misery?" Lillian looked dismayed. "Sorry about that. If you still want me to, I'll come with you."

Her smile returned. "Come on. This visit may be very different than what you expect."

They rode up in the elevator in silence, their arms barely touching. Adam was feeling the out of body distancing creeping over him, that mode of being there, but not really being there. Ed Bennett was on his back, his head and neck in an immobilizing brace, with a tube running to a bottle full of dark concentrated urine hanging under his bed. He was breathing on his own and came to life at the sight of Lillian. He smiled, slowly reached out for Lillian's hand and Adam thought, "This prick is going to recover."

Bennett was clean shaven, his hair was cut short. He looked like the all-American boy, not as Adam remembered. He saw the tattoo on the lower part of his neck. The head of a snake that slithered up from his chest. Adam was thinking maybe this was another chance to chop its head off. When he saw Ed Bennett open his mouth and say, "Hi Lillian," he had the impulse to finish the job.

"Hi Ed, I see you have more movement in your arms...that's great...I'd like you to meet Adam Burns. He's the guy that put you here...the one you shot in the belly."

Adam was stunned. She laid it all out without any frills — he didn't know what to say to Ed Bennett. There was an awkward silence as they stared at each other. Finally Ed Bennett said, "I don't know what to say except I'm sorry I shot you...I'm glad you're OK."

Adam stood frozen, holding his tongue from saying he was sorry he missed and sorry he was still alive. Lillian was the only reason he didn't. He let his silence punctuate his rage. It was not concealed in his tone, when he said,

"I don't know why I came here with Lillian...maybe because I didn't want to disappoint her. I'm not as forgiving as she is or as good a person as she...I'm not sorry for what I did to you. You got less than you deserved." He shut down and turned to Lillian. "Sorry Lillian, I'll see you later."

He left simmering with anger at Ed Bennett. By the time he hit the street he was fuming with rage and not too happy with Lillian. In the not so distant past he would have found a bar, let the booze and cigarettes soothe his mood, instead, he walked letting that steely iciness form its protective coat. He didn't need anyone or anything. Maybe this was the time for Lillian and him to part. He took a deep breath — walked on — his mind blank. Then out of the blue, he felt his insides fall out. He had flashes of his guys lying next to their intestines, except it was him, his insides floating on a pool of blood. He wandered aimlessly and found himself at the ER. The thought of losing Lillian was more than he could bear and he needed to make sure they were still together. The voice of Dr. Goodman's measured tones intruded, "Why would you think you would lose her?" Or maybe he would be asking, "Why were you thinking of leaving her?"

He tried to snap out of it. He was about to drive himself nuts — he couldn't let it go. He was so preoccupied he didn't realize he was approaching the front doors to the ER and was retrieved from his own belly button by three cops who were drinking coffee and having a smoke.

"Hey doc, how ya doing?"

Adam was a bit of a celebrity since he took Ed Bennett down and made national news. "Pretty good…almost back to normal."

"We hear the shooter is recovering…too bad, it could've save the state a lot of dough."

Adam came back with, "Well you can't have everything."

It was a few hours before Lillian got off so he bummed a cigarette and listened to what cops talk about when they have time on their hands. He was expecting war stories of the street, instead got an earful of baseball, women, families and what they were going to do on their days off. Listening to the unburdened chatter of these three guys who sounded like they were engaged in life, he started to feel more fucked-up than ever. It seemed he would never feel at peace with himself. He thanked the cop for the cigarette, told him he really ought to stop smoking and started to walk.

Walking was not as numbing as drinking himself into a stupor — it helped to keep moving. Any relief was short-lived. He couldn't get rid of the image of the way Ed Bennett lit up when he saw Lillian. He wanted to kill him. Then this crazy thought took over — "I saved him from being a killer and no one did that for me and that's the reason I killed all those people — people I never knew and no one ever tried to stop me and I'm still alive — I didn't die and there's no one to forgive me."

Adam was walking in circles ending up outside his apartment building. His mailbox was full with bills, advertisements and a notice from the University Apartments. He would have to vacate his apartment since he was no longer affiliated with the University. Adam was brought back to his senses by the realities of life. His first thought was he'd move in with Lillian. The second thought came from somewhere outside of himself saying, that will never happen.

There were phone messages on his new message recorder that he tends to forget he has. One from his folks, a message from Dr. Martin and one from Tom. His parents were fine and wanted to know how he was doing. His Mother ended with, "Goddamn it Adam, remember the last time we saw you, you were recovering from surgery. You need to call us." His Mom never needed permission to say how she felt.

Dr. Martin said the chancellor wanted to meet with him and the board of directors of the University. He wanted to speak with Adam before the meeting.

Tom's message was to let Adam know he had spoken to the chancellor. He told him the conditions were non-negotiable and any further communications should be with Dr. Burns. Tom also suggested Adam get a pager and answering service. He wanted Adam to let him know when he was ready to come to the Foundation office in Washington, to meet the people he'd be working with. Tom sounded confident Adam was going to accept the job. Adam thought maybe Tom knew him better than he knew himself. The only thing he knew for sure, was he wanted to see Lillian and needed to see Dr. G.

He changed clothes, grabbed his daypack and was almost out the door when he remembered he hadn't called Dr. Goodman. He also left his keys on the table next to the phone almost locking himself out of the apartment. He managed to crack a smile over his ambivalence it didn't make a dent on his mood. He left a message with Dr. Goodman's answering service asking for an appointment. Then he checked the telephone recorder manual and wrote down the instructions of how to access the machine from a remote phone. He managed another smile when he remembered the salesman

I don't who recall she is

telling him how easy it was to use the machine, even a child could do it. At this point he wasn't sure he could find his way to the ER all by himself.

When he got to the ER he realized he was a half hour early. Lillian was with a patient, so he went to the staff lounge to call to Dr. Martin. Mrs. Beaman's welcoming voice sent all his demons into hiding, then Dr. Martin helped keep them there.

"Hello Adam. Thanks so much for getting back to me so promptly. The reason I wanted to talk with you is I have a feeling Aubrey is going to ask me to negotiate with you and Tom for a more multi-use building."

"Well Dr. Martin, Tom told me he spoke with Dr. Lowell and made sure he understood the terms of the gift were non-negotiable. He also told me to pull the plug on this offer if we were going to have an on-going fight with the University. I've been thinking that it would be a lot easier to take the project off campus. We can still affiliate with your department."

"I think you may be right. I'll get back to you after the meeting."

Adam could sense the steel in Dr. Martin's last remark and thought Aubrey Lowell is in for a surprise. He hoped he wasn't in for a surprise from Lillian. Adam ran out of distractions, just sat there anticipating the worst and promptly fell asleep. He heard a rifle bolt slam shut and bolted upright to see Lillian standing at her locker changing clothes.

"Oh sorry, Adam, I was trying to be quiet so as not to wake you." She planted herself on his lap, kissed his face awake and said, "I feel badly dragging you along to see Ed Bennett. I didn't think about your having some feelings about him almost blowing you away."

"I was thinking more about what he might have done to you...I wasn't about to forgive him." He ran his finger over her lips. "I hope you're not mad at me for saying what I did and flying out of there. I know your being able to talk with him, maybe to even forgive him, is a giant step for you. I have to remind myself as much as I love you we're two separate people."

"It's a good reminder for me too."

It would be hard for Adam to describe the relief he felt. All the fragmented thoughts solidified. He felt whole and bursting with love for this woman who he thought he lost just a few moments ago. They swam, talked, had dinner and made love.

———

It was still strange to Adam — how swiftly his mood shifts. All the urgency of needing to see Dr. Goodman was a distant memory, barely recoverable. He still wanted to see him but now it felt it was more like a social call. When he walked into his office he felt he was stumbling over his feet, like a little kid in the awkward stage. He sat with a simple-minded smile waiting for something to happen.

Dr. Goodman said, "When I spoke to you on the phone you sounded agitated, now you look serene as if you don't have a care in the world."

At first Adam thought he was mixing him up with some other patient. Then the whole scene with Ed Bennett came to mind. The feelings came charging back as he told him what happened. "I couldn't believe Lillian wanting to forgive him. I wanted to kill the bastard...I pretty much told him so."

"What did you say to him?"

"I didn't know why I was there...I wasn't as nice as Lillian...he got less than he deserved.....then I left."

"Why did you go to see him?"

"I don't know. I didn't want to go."

"But you did."

"To please Lillian. I don't know." He was quiet and just looked at Dr. G.

"Adam, you keep saying you don't know. I think you've got some ideas why you went to see Bennett."

"Oh yeah. What do you think they are?" He didn't answer. "So what are you thinking, Doc?"

"I'm thinking that you're being a smart ass...provocative because it's hard for you to face something about yourself."

"And I'm thinking I want to break your neck, like I did Ed Bennett...I'd like to go back...finish the job...I'm thinking why the fuck is she paying so much attention to him/I'm a victim too." He stopped. He wanted to take the last part back. It just popped out. He never thought of himself as a victim — it didn't sit well with him.

"You are a victim. I know you don't like to see yourself that way. You lost half of one lung, almost lost your head and have enough screws in your leg to stock a hardware store. You're a victim of war. You live with the memory of John Phillips' head in your lap. You're carrying around a load of guilt over every Marine you lost... everyone you killed or ordered strikes on. You can't get from under the black cloud."

He was stunned. Goodman was right. He didn't know what to say. "So what can I do about it?"

"You're doing it...a little at a time...you need to come here regularly so we can work on this."

"I'll be coming here forever...I'll never get free...I need to set Lillian loose. She doesn't need me hanging around her neck........you'll get tired of listening to all my shit too."

"So I won't be able to stand you. Maybe you shouldn't come more regularly?"

There was a long silence where they looked at each other. Dr. Goodman said,

"Tell me what you're thinking and feeling?"

"I was thinking I make fifty grand a year now. I should be paying your full fee."

"Oh, so then I'd be able to tolerate seeing you?"

Adam started to laugh. "OK, if I pay you more it would ease the burden of seeing me."

"I think you should pay my full fee because that's the reasonable and fair thing to do. I also think you should come here regularly...I would like to see you five times a week."

"Wow...that's overkill. Why five times a week?"

"Nobody will be killed. We can work more intensely with less time between sessions."

"I'm not going to lie on the couch."

"You can stand on your head in the corner if it helps us work together. You need to be here."

"I may have to be away on business. Will you charge me for missed sessions?"

"I would expect we would treat each other fairly. We can talk about it when you miss a session."

"What if I'm late for a session?...oh shit...I can't stop this bullshit questioning. I think for the first time I can remember I'm really scared."

"That's a good start, Adam."

———

Right from the beginning of the five day a week therapy, Adam was on the couch. He just walked in, got on the couch and said,

"I guess I'm in analysis now."

Dr. G said, "We've been analyzing since the first day we met. The difference is that you're horizontal and coming more often."

"I've always known you were a bit of a smart ass...we're pretty well matched."

It didn't take long for Adam to shed his Marine armor, although it was always handy. His mood seemed to swing between what for him was a deep depression, hardly noticeable to anyone who didn't know him well, never-the-less excruciatingly painful, and a mania, equally well disguised in a wise-ass sarcasm that could be charming as well as lethal. At least he thought he was lethal. He was angry, simmering most of the time and started to have blinding headaches. He also thought maybe he needed some Lithium. When he told Dr. G that. He said,

"Tell me what's going on inside you, that makes you think Lithium would help."

He thought for a moment. His voice became calm, quiet and his words came out measured — studied. "I think I need Lithium because I think I'm going crazy...sometimes I wonder what it would feel like to put a gun in my mouth and blow the top of my head off...it's like I would still be here and would then know what it feels like...I see myself walking around looking in the mirror...seeing myself without a top on my head........then I think I'll join the Navy...become a Navy doc...get assigned to a Marine battalion or the Seals...these aren't thoughts I have...I'm actually there...not dreams...actually taking care of the wounded with no top to my head...........I forgot what you asked me...Oh, I remember...Lithium...as crazy as I feel I also feel exhilarated.... like I don't want to stop feeling nuts...then I want to imitate Tom when he was nuts...then I think I'm really like Tom...maybe Lithium wouldn't help...maybe a phenothiazine or ECT....... So what do you think Doc?"

"Well, Adam, I don't think Lithium or any of the phenothiazines are indicated, but maybe some ECT would do the trick."

"I think your losing your mind. Are you serious?"

"No I'm not...are you serious?"

"You really are a wise-ass prick, Doc."

"I asked you not to call me Doc. You've called me Doc twice today, and several times last week."

"So?"

"So, I think you want to blow your top at me but your afraid you'll kill me. You want me to restrain you with meds or shock treatment."

"I think your out in left field some place...not everything I say here has to do with you." Adam started to get a headache and noticed he was sweating. When he checked his pulse, it was so fast he couldn't count it. He couldn't speak. He didn't know how long he was quiet. Then he started to treat Dr. G to a dose of humorous sarcasm, but stopped himself.

"I don't know why I'm so angry...I started to have these headaches about the time we began meeting five times a week."

"I remember your telling me for the first time you can remember, you were feeling scared. Do you think being scared has some connection to feeling so angry?"

"I forgot that I said that...I...I was going to say I wasn't scared, but I was. I remember asking you all kinds of nit-picking questions...I know this sounds crazy but all the time I was in Korea I never remember feeling scared...I think I must've been at times but never felt it...I think I've told you that before but it's true. It was like I was on a job and had my work cut out for me........Oh shit...the kid who's throat I slit...I can't shake that." He stopped talking and could feel the anger simmering inside. "I don't know why I'm coming here. This shit will never go away no matter how much I talk about it. You keep pushing my nose in it. I don't think the more I talk about it...relive it...the better I'll be. I'll just get deeper and deeper into it...twice is enough...I don't need a third tour. I don't give a shit what you say. I'm not going back there again." He was enraged, shouting and was about to walk out when Dr. Goodman said,

"So that's why you're so angry with me. I'm sending you back into dangerous territory...putting you in harms way to do the dirty work."

"What the fuck is the matter with you? It's not about you...it's about whoever started this senseless stupid war and sent us to kill innocent people. For what? I bought it all...not only bought it but gloried in it...I didn't have enough killing the first time so I had to have double dips…now I'm a big fucking war hero…I love it and I hate it and I can't live with what I've done." He sat up and looked at Dr. Goodman. "So I'm all fucked up…I don't know what to do about it…that's why I thought of Lithium…that's why I think of blowing the top of my head off." He sat in silence for a long time, waiting for the hour to end and his rage to retreat to the shadows. "OK, I am angry at you…I do feel like your sending me on a third tour, but I'm more angry at myself for going along with it…why in the world would I go to Annapolis then the Marines…what the hell am I doing here?"

He left feeling pathetic and despicable. He thought, "I'm finished. I'm never going back there."

■■■

Well, he kept going back. In fact, he never missed a session, except when he had to travel for his new job. He never got back on the couch for he needed to see Dr. Goodman's reactions to what he was saying and feeling. Adam watched Goodman like a hawk for any sign of revulsion, as he was into a loathing of himself. Over the next year he lived through the war over and over, only on this tour he was hooked up to what he felt, and for the most part it took place in Dr. G's office. The fear, revulsion and rage was often more than Adam could bear as he was able to allow the memories to creep out of hiding. Sometimes it felt as if the dam shattered and he felt like he was drowning in blood.

He could feel the warm blood pulsing through his fingers when he slit the sentry's throat and could feel the blade going through his trachea. He could hear the kid he carried on his back humming the Marine hymn in his ear, as his blood warmed his back propelling him to keep moving. He had long forgotten asking John Phillips to scrub the blood off his back and how he kept telling Adam his back was clean. He remembered every kid he sent home in a body bag, and the wrenching pain as he wrote a letter to their family.

One day he was telling Dr. Goodman how hardened Marines would vomit their guts as they stepped over bodies of blown apart women and children when he noticed tears streaming down his cheeks. Adam knew those tears were the remnants of his war. That's when Adam knew that John Phillips' head would always be in his lap. He could never get his hands clean enough no matter how many times he washed them. He would always be haunted by the nameless ones. The horrors of war were bubbling in his brain, making him nauseous, blinding his vision and at this point in his therapy it didn't take much to trigger a headache that made him want to scream.

It was hard for Adam to believe therapy was helping or he was getting better, so when Lillian told him he seemed to be more at one with himself he chalked it off to her wishful thinking. Actually, outside of his time with Dr. Goodman, he knew she was right. He didn't feel as guarded and not every new encounter was a potential fight to the death. He wouldn't call it a cure but he was feeling less shattered. He had more free energy. It's like not having to play offense and defense simultaneously. His dreams were losing their power. In his sleep he seemed to know they were just dreams

It was

which made what he was dreaming about part of his past and not alive in the here and now. He found it a huge relief to not dread going to sleep. It's also amazing to Adam that his headaches were now confined to his therapy sessions. He'd have a blinding headache he would talk through, while holding his head in his hands, and as soon as he left Dr. G's office the headache was gone. John Phillips' head was always in his lap, and talking about it had no effect on the headaches. *hadn't*

In life outside of the therapy hour, the haunting feeling he hasn't been able to shake is a fear all the joys *was* of his life would somehow come to an abrupt end. Not just an abrupt end but a violent end. Like he was living on borrowed time. He didn't know how many times he talked about this in therapy but nothing seemed to ablate the foreboding sense of impending catastrophe. Lillian would tire of him, or Lillian would die — with her death his will to live would slowly and painfully erode. It wasn't in the front of his mind twenty-four *ed* hours a day, but it hovers in the background, often buried out of sight, festering and contaminating like a slow leak of sewerage.

After almost two years of seeing Dr. G five times a week, except for the headaches and the feeling he was living on borrowed time, he was doing pretty well. He was convinced it was as good as it was going to get, and brought up the idea of stopping treatment or at least cutting back to one or two times a week.

It was on a Monday, he had just flown in from Washington, DC, where he had been at a meeting with Tom, Elizabeth and the Foundation staff. He took a cab to Dr. G's office and arrived, with suitcase in hand, as he opened his door.

"Hi Adam, how was your trip?"

"It was fine…I'm lucky to be here. I was supposed to fly back yesterday and would have been on the flight that crash landed in Philadelphia. I think ten or twenty people got off the plane before it burst into flames. I live a charmed life."

"Oh yeah…you are lucky. I'm happy you changed your plans."

"It's because of Tom…there was a huge banquet on Saturday, honoring Elizabeth for all she's done and for her birthday…then Tom decided we ought to have a more intimate celebration on Sunday, with just family…we had dinner with Sophie, Tom, Elizabeth and me…it felt so good to be thought of as family. It was a lovely time together." He went on talking about the banquet and Sunday dinner, until Dr. Goodman asked,

"I wonder if you have some feelings about the close call you just had?"

"Well I told you I was lucky…I could've been on that plane and probably wouldn't be sitting here now." They sat looking at each other and he wondered what the hell is Goodman thinking? "So I had a near miss…so what? I had lots of near misses. I'm glad I wasn't on that plane." Then it hit him — out of the blue — right between the eyes. It was as if he had never talked about John Phillips. He was flooded with feelings and couldn't talk. That was the near miss. If he had been sitting where John was and John where he was, it would've been Adam's head in John's lap. Adam had always thought that John saved his life but never allowed himself to think he was glad it was John and not him. He sat, so flooded with his shame that he couldn't move or talk. He was staring at the floor, avoiding looking at Dr. G.

"You've been staring at the floor for over five minutes. I don't know what you're thinking but you look like you just lost your best friend."

He just sat there. The tears flowing, his voice had vanished. He must have used a half a box of tissues which he had wadded up, twisting them, like he was wringing out the feelings. When Adam left, he managed to mumble that maybe he would be able to talk tomorrow.

———

Lillian convinced Adam to move in with her. It didn't take much convincing. They worked out a way to share the 2500 square feet of her apartment. Adam paid a respectable rent which satisfied his need to pay his way. It was an ideal setup. Their love expanded into a loving friendship without losing the excitement of being lovers, but the fear of losing Lillian was always in the background. It seemed to find a permanent place in the layers of Adam's mind. He thought today was the day she would find him too disgusting to be with. If he told her what happened in his session with Dr. G, she would never be able to love him. So he lied when she asked why he looked so burdened. Not an outright lie, more a half-truth, or half the story, like he never realized how guilty he felt about surviving the war when so many didn't.

It must have sounded hollow to her for she gave Adam one of those, there's more-to-this look, or at least Adam thought she did, and it all came spilling out. It didn't take much. Just a look. He told her everything he felt so ashamed and guilty about, then waited for her verdict. She gathered him to her, held him, rounding his back in a soothing-soft-path of reassuring pats. He tried to squirm away but she held firm until he could overcome the guilt of being comforted despite his crimes.

Her reaction gave Adam the courage to once more tell Dr. Goodman the gory details of finding John's head in his lap. This time he could tell him how he felt sitting there with John staring at him. The second mortar round didn't come as soon as he led himself to believe. He didn't know how long he sat feeling the blood flow out of John's head, his eyes open, jaw clenched as if he had anticipated the blow that separated him from himself. It wasn't terror or horror Adam felt, it was total, massive disbelief and before he could feel anything else or grasped what had happened the merciful curtain came down. The second round came in and he vanished into coma until the curtain lifted to reveal the smiling faces of his loving mother and father who were treated to a vile outburst of profanity. Sometimes he wondered if he was really in a comatose state or into a forced hibernation to escape for a time, in order to tolerate living — living with the thought he was glad it was John and not him.

It took a while to be able to let himself off the hook he created. The black cloud turned a light shade of grey, all loud noises were not as potentially dangerous, the compulsion to wash his hands was not ever-present, the dreams were not as frequent and rarely woke him from sleep. They took on a different repetitive theme of his being entangled or ensnared in fibrous webs, or red sucking mud and being pulled free by some vague force, a blurred figure or face. As he became untangled from the ravages of war he experienced a freedom that had eluded him. It was the kind of free spirit he felt when his dad let go of the bicycle seat and he was soaring on his own. A powerful curative force in his therapy was knowing Dr. Goodman would stick with him and not let go of the seat until the finishing line was in sight. Underlying it all, was being in love with and loving Lillian and being able to allow her to love him.

The guilt for being alive was fading which felt a bit strange at first. The lightness and soaring gave way to more even ground. The scars of war were becoming less tender, still there, but more often than not, lacking in significance. He knew in his bones, the reason he was in a better place, was the healing power of being loved and cared about. Knowing about himself was important, but being loved was what made lifting the veil of the burden of guilt possible. He was convinced of that.

■ ■ ■

Adam wrote a letter to John Phillips' parents, asking if he could visit with them. He wasn't exactly sure why. He knew he wasn't going to confess his sin. He did want them to know he valued John, his friendship and the memory of him. It would make Adam feel better and he hoped it would somehow be of help to them. He knew he would always have a mixture of feelings about being the survivor, but was more at peace with the luck of the draw.

A few weeks went by when Adam received a letter from John's sister. His letter had been forwarded to her. John's parents died two years ago, within six months of each other. She said they never got over losing their youngest child. He remembered John's mother telling him, John was buried in his dress blues with all his medals and how proud she was of him. Adam said a silent thanks to whoever reattached John's head and sent a short note to John's sister.

He was at a point where he could take the spotlight off himself and be more present in the present, especially for Lillian. This tough, compassionate, loving woman, stuck with him through all his wrestling matches with himself, which too often spilled over on her. They sometimes thought they were too much alike, rough around the edges — not eager to back down. They still have some knockdowns over Ed Bennett. Adam couldn't stomach her wanting to visit this guy who tried to rape her, hunted her down, only to almost blow Adam away. He knew she was working something out within herself. It served to quiet his waters, most of the time, but he couldn't resist a gentle needle oblivious to a blazing no trespass sign, until Lillian screamed,

"Goddamn it Adam. Enough…this isn't about you or Ed Bennett. It's about me…what I have to do to be at peace with myself…what do I have to do to get you to understand?"

The waters were still, not even a ripple. "You got my attention Lillie babe. I do understand. I'm truly sorry."

She kissed him. "Only my father can call me Lillie babe."

The Ed Bennett issue was put to rest. In a few weeks Ed Bennett was put to rest. He developed a fulminating kidney infection and pneumonia. His vital systems shut down. He said his goodbye to Lillian, the only person who visited him, talked with him and listened. He asked for forgiveness and hoped Adam would forgive him. Lillian prospered from her relationship with Ed Bennett. It made forgiving him an easier road for Adam, but he was glad Bennett was out of their lives.

———

Lillian's ideas for the delivery of emergency medical care, and the training curriculum she had developed, was becoming a national model for the emerging specialty of emergency medicine. She received several offers from some prestigious academic centers. When she was offered the position of Chair of Emergency Medicine at George Washington University Medical Center she was delighted. Adam shared her delight. It wasn't lost on either one of them, that she was being recognized for her contributions to a field of medicine which dealt with all matters of trauma.

They found a townhouse in Washington which ended Adam's weekly commute to the Wittenbourne Foundation office. So far they've managed to get to work on bicycles and will take taxies in bad weather. Navigating through the traffic on a bike was a bit challenging, but beat owning a car.

Adam withdrew the offer to the University and found a site two blocks from the University Health Sciences campus. They broke ground on the Mark Wittenbourne Center for the Behavioral Sciences.

Dr. Martin was named director and chair of the board of directors. He and Adam were pleased not to have the chancellor to deal with.

It was bittersweet saying goodbye to Steven Goodman, Adam's therapist, teacher, listener, fellow trauma sufferer and strong advocate. Of the people who have had their lives disrupted by severe trauma, who Adam had been close to these past few years, Dr. Goodman *was* the one he knew least about. He could imagine what he experienced in WWII, and guessed that an important part of his dealing with it, *was* is tied to the work he has chosen. It was time to move on but wrenching to leave. Adam knew Dr. Goodman's door was always open.

Over the next few years Adam worked and consulted almost daily with Elizabeth. They visited all the projects the Foundation was involved in, which gave her a chance to see if Adam was up to taking them over and Adam the opportunity to see if he wanted to. He knew Elizabeth was every bit as bright and accomplished as Tom. He found she also had the touch of maturity and wisdom that comes to someone who has not only survived the unthinkable, but has carried love ones to safety. On several trips, especially in Africa, she shared how she learned to live and grow with a psychotic mother and an alcoholic father who was manic-depressive. The extreme conditions that the children had in some of the villages they visited, resonated in some ways with the emotional poverty and chaos she experienced. She and Mark were saved by a protective nanny, and they in turned saved Tom. Now, some of the children in extreme need, are being saved by Elizabeth, Tom and the Foundation.

On a return trip from Africa, they stopped-over in France to meet with a group of doctors and journalists who had submitted a grant request. They were starting a non-profit to provide medical care to victims of war and other catastrophes. Adam thought they should support this group. He was talking non-stop, excited about the French group, as well as what could be done for veterans, victims of war, and the war that was escalating in Vietnam. Elizabeth patiently heard him out and said,

"If you became CEO of the Foundation you could put the money where your mouth is…do you want the job?"

The wind went out of Adam's sails. His silence was louder than any words.

"The Foundation is a two billion dollar operation…I don't have the experience in finance to run it…I think you should stay CEO…I don't have the expertise."

"Well Adam, the Foundation is closer to a ten billion dollar operation…I wouldn't have asked you if I didn't think you could do it…the CEO hires a Chief Financial Officer…we have a pretty good one now…don't forget we always have Tom in the wings…an effective CEO doesn't just run things he leads with a vision…you're a leader…a natural."

"Being a company commander is not like being the general."

"If we had more generals like you we wouldn't be repeating the same mistake in Vietnam as we did in Korea…let it sink in…talk it over with Lillian…with Tom…then we can talk more."

That's what he did, talk. He talked with Lillian and with Tom and with Elizabeth and the more he talked the more he liked the idea of being able to put money where his mouth is. He was overflowing with ideas — now he would have the vehicle to test them out. Adam felt he was the luckiest guy in the world — to top it off there was no dark cloud.

Adam became CEO of the Wittenbourne Foundation. Elizabeth and Tom held Adam's hand as he learned to be an effective leader of a workforce of over two hundred people. He chaired committees, evaluated grants, supervised project managers, decided which non-profits to support and a hundred other things he never gave a thought to. To his amazement, he was thriving and enjoying the hell out of the job.

———

Tom and Sophie were a continuing surprise to Adam, and maybe to each other. This gay man and vivacious, talented woman looked to be a committed couple. Tom's love for Sophie was only surpassed by Sophie's love for Tom. They came to their own special private arrangement about how they would be with each other and surprised everyone when they announced their upcoming marriage and Sophie's pregnancy.

Tom asked Adam to be his best man, and when he did he said, "You know I'm not bisexual...Sophie knows as much as I love her I'm not sexually aroused by her...God knows she's tried everything...when we decided we wanted to have a baby together she ruled out artificial insemination...she wanted me inside her...she told me to think of whatever it takes to get me aroused. The first person I fantasized I was having sex with was Mark. Then Mark turned into you...that's when I was able to have an orgasm.......I don't know why I had to tell you this....I guess I want you to know that you helped me make a baby...I hope I haven't embarrassed you."

Adam kissed Tom — a tender kiss on the lips, "I love you Tom. I'm honored to be able to help you make a baby."

Tom passed the tissues to Adam. They toasted their baby, which turned out to be babies. A boy and a girl. They couldn't ask for better parents. They were the luckiest kids in the world.

■ ■ ■

Made in the USA
Charleston, SC
05 September 2010